THE MAN

DOCTOR #2

E. L. TODD

Hartwick Publishing

The Man

CONTENTS

1. Pepper   1
2. Colton   17
3. Pepper   31
4. Colton   49
5. Pepper   59
6. Colton   69
7. Pepper   73
8. Colton   79
9. Pepper   89
10. Pepper   105
11. Pepper   129
12. Colton   141
13. Pepper   159
14. Colton   165
15. Pepper   175
16. Colton   189
17. Pepper   193
18. Colton   211
19. Pepper   219
20. Colton   235
21. Colton   245
22. Pepper   253
23. Colton   267

Also by E. L. Todd   281

1

PEPPER

I left my apartment with the bag on my arm. It was full of paper plates and plastic utensils, a necessity Finn and Colton would need now that they'd just moved in to their new place. They had furniture and the TV, but they were still missing the basic necessities. Just when I locked the door and turned away, I spotted a man outside Colton's old door.

Tall, muscular, and blond, he was dressed in workout shorts and a t-shirt. The sweat stains indicated he'd just been to the gym. He had nice calves and thick arms, the kind where the veins were noticeable across the skin. He had his keys in his hand, but instead of unlocking the door right away, he looked at me.

Whoa, I didn't realize my new neighbor was so hot.

I was bummed when Colton left because his presence gave me so much comfort, but this didn't feel so bad. And maybe he was straight. He stared at me like he was straight. But he was also too good-looking to be true. "So, you're the new guy?" I came closer to him, keeping up my confidence even though the jitters were in my body.

"Damon." He extended his hand to shake mine. "Sorry, I'm a little sweaty..."

I took his hand. "Who isn't?"

His eyes fell slightly at the comment.

Wow, that was a weird thing to say. "So, uh, let me know if you need anything. Are you new to Seattle?"

"No. Newly divorced."

"Ooh...I'm so sorry." I meant it from the bottom of my heart because divorce was brutal. I never thought I would get through it. It'd been nine months since I signed the papers, but the memories still haunted me. "I'm divorced too. It sucks."

He chuckled. "That's an understatement. I'm sorry, by the way."

"It's okay. It's been about nine months, so I'm in a good place. But getting there...took forever. What about you?"

"Just divorced," he said. "We signed the papers last week."

"I'm sorry..." He was in the worst phase. "But I can promise you, it gets easier. It doesn't seem like it now, but it will."

"Thanks. You're my favorite neighbor."

"Have you met the others?"

"No." He smiled. "But I don't think I need to."

I WALKED to the front door and rang the doorbell. His beautiful home on Escala looked even more glorious with the lights shining in the window. It was so quiet, the occasional sound of a boat horn sounding in the distance.

Footsteps sounded before Finn opened the door, shirtless and covered in ink. It was only fifty degrees that evening, but the temperature never dissuaded him. At six-three, he stood over me, the shadow on his jawline adding a darker element of color to his face. He looked at me with those glorious blue eyes, crafting a silent conversation between us no one else could hear. He didn't greet me with a word as he opened the door wider and allowed me inside.

"Colton invited me over. Is that okay?" I came inside and wiped my boots on the rug.

"You're welcome here anytime."

"Be careful what you say...I might show up every night around dinnertime."

"Fine with me." He walked through the foyer, past the staircase, and into the open floor plan that showed the kitchen and living room in the same space. The TV was on, showing a football game. "You want a beer?"

"Sure." I set the bag on the counter and pulled out the contents. "I got you a little gift."

"Yeah?" He twisted off the cap then set the beer beside me on the counter.

I pulled out the plates and utensils. "It's not much, but I know you don't have any dishes yet. This should get you by until you do."

A slight smile cracked his lips. "Colton is picking up dinner, so this is perfect."

I turned around and examined his black leather sofa and the large TV mounted on the wall. A gray rug was on the hardwood floor and the fireplace had flames burning, bringing heat into the space. "It looks nice."

"Of course it does. You picked everything out."

"I think it suits your personality."

"And what kind of personality do I have?"

I turned back around and looked at him, doing my best not to let my eyes drift down over his perfectly sculpted body. Black ink covered most of his skin but didn't diminish his muscularity. My fingertips would always remember how hard he was, how his muscles felt like rocks rather than living tissue. The military dog tags hung around his neck where they always rested, shiny pieces of metal showing his identity. He'd been out of the military for several months now, but he still didn't remove them. "Quiet, masculine, earthy..."

"Good. I thought you were gonna say asshole."

I slapped his arm playfully. "Never." The backs of my fingers brushed against his bicep, and the short interaction was enough for me to feel the warmth, to feel the strong structure of his body. Like any other time we touched, I felt the fire ignite. When I met his look again, the desire was there, my own reflected in his beautiful eyes. I turned away and cleared my throat. "What is Colton getting?"

"Pizza."

"They don't deliver?"

He shook his head. "Not this place. And he says it's the best."

"Must be Coopers," I said. "And he's right, they are the best."

He continued to stand close to me, the smell of his body soap fragrant in the air. He never wore cologne. His natural smell was hypnotic enough. "I'm not working on Thursday. You want to help me pick out everything for the kitchen?"

Any extra time I spent with this man felt wrong, when my thoughts were always dictated by the obvious heat between us. We managed to remain platonic when we were alone together, so hopefully, it would stay that way. Finn seemed to have strong discipline when it came to all things, so I probably didn't need to worry about anything happening. As long as I didn't make a move, everything would be fine. "Sure."

"Thanks. Otherwise, I'll just pick out the first thing

I see."

"And if that's a flower pattern, it would clash with this house."

He shrugged. "They could be pink with kittens, and I probably wouldn't care."

Because this man was so brutishly masculine that it didn't matter how feminine his dishes were. He could wear all pink and still pick up any woman he wanted. He was secure in his masculinity to the point where nothing could challenge the testosterone he constantly pumped into the air. "Have your parents come around yet?" I took a drink of the ice-cold beer he gave me.

He shook his head.

"Have you talked to them?"

"My mom calls me every day. She doesn't mention Colt at all."

I raised an eyebrow. "That's pretty impressive, considering he's your brother and your roommate."

He shrugged. "She just needs some time."

"Does she normally call you every day?"

"When I was in the military, it wasn't possible. But she would write me a letter every single day. I served ten years in the military...that's a lot of letters. I'm not a big talker, but I'll let her have her way for a while."

I smiled. "That's sweet."

"She's my mom." He grabbed a bottle of scotch and poured a glass. "I kinda owe her for everything."

He was so quiet and gloomy most of the time, but when it came to his parents, he was respectful and kind. He only showed his heart for his family, like when Colton was discriminated against at work. Finn was there in a heartbeat. "Maybe she'll become less clingy as time goes on."

He chuckled. "I doubt it. But that would be nice."

"Well, when you get married, she's going to have to."

He took a drink, the muscles of his jaw and throat working to get the liquor down. "I'll never get married, so that won't be a problem. And even if I did, I'm not interested in being with a woman who doesn't understand the importance of family."

I smiled again. "You're just a big ol' sweetheart, aren't you?"

"No. I just understand respect better than most people." He finished his glass then poured another.

"Do you think you could talk to your mom on Colton's behalf? Maybe calm her down?"

"Eventually. I'm gonna give her the chance to do the right thing first. I would never take that away from her."

"But do you think she'll do the right thing?"

He held the glass near his stomach and regarded me for nearly a full minute. "Every letter she ever wrote me talked about Colton. I know she loves him as much as she loves me. I'm not the favorite—despite what Colton thinks. If anything, he's the favorite. That's why she's taking this so hard. She had high expectations for him."

"But he didn't hurt those expectations by being gay."

"That's not what bothers her." He held my look for a long time. "Losing you is what bothers her. And I don't blame her."

AFTER WE DEMOLISHED the pizza in the boxes on the couches, Colton turned to me. "Why didn't you invite Jax over? Doesn't he live up the street?"

Finn sat on the other couch with both of his arms across the back of the couch. He took up every inch possible like a wild bear. His eyes had been glued to the TV, but they flicked to us at the mention of Jax.

I hadn't told Colton the truth since he'd had such a hard week. "We kinda broke up..."

"What?" Colton asked, dumbfounded. He was about to take a drink of his beer but returned it to the coaster instead, because this was clearly more important than his need for alcohol. "When did this happen?"

"Last week."

"Ooh...are you okay?" Colton gave me that look of sympathy he'd been showing since the day we met. He really cared about how I felt, really cared if I was hurting. He would take all my pain if he could.

"Yeah, I'm fine." I was sad in the beginning because it was a shame to lose a man over Colton, but as time went by, I realized I should be with someone who understood my situation. I needed him to be close with Colton just as I was, to understand he wasn't a threat in the least. I did miss getting laid, though. Jax was good in the sack. "It wasn't meant to be. Ever since the beginning, that relationship always turned in a direction I didn't want it to go."

"True," Colton said in agreement.

"Relationships shouldn't be hard." Finn spoke as he looked at the TV. "If you're with the right person, it should be the easiest thing in the world."

"And how would you know?" Colton countered. "Your longest relationship is four hours."

Finn shifted his gaze to him. "A romantic relationship shouldn't be any different from a platonic one. You never fight with your best friend, so why should you fight with your lover? Attraction gets in the way of that, makes people not think clearly. Which is why a man and a woman should just be able to fuck and go their separate ways."

Colton listened to him then slowly turned to me. "You know, that actually makes sense."

"Of course it does." He grabbed his scotch and took a drink. "That's all Pepper wanted, a physical relationship. But the asshole tried to make it complicated when he shouldn't have. This is entirely his fault."

Colton nodded. "I agree with that."

"He's not an asshole," I corrected. "He just...wanted more than I could give."

"Because he's selfish." Finn looked at me, his blue eyes staring me down with their usual intensity. He was sweet just minutes ago, but whenever Jax was mentioned, he turned into a colder version of himself. "Men shouldn't be selfish—and especially not in bed."

"So he broke up with you?" Colton asked.

I nodded.

"Why?"

I shrugged, trying to find an answer that wasn't too much of a lie. "He wanted something more serious, and I didn't. That's pretty much the story...in a nutshell." I couldn't tell Colton the truth because he would feel so guilty. None of this would have happened if he hadn't slept over that one night. It was better that he didn't know the truth.

"It sounds like he was a bit obsessed with you," Colton said. "I guess that's a good problem to have."

No, that wasn't the problem at all. "Maybe..."

Colton patted my thigh. "Let me know if you need anything. I'd set you up with someone if I knew anyone..."

Finn stared at him.

"That's okay," I said. "I'm not anxious to get back in

the dating world again. I was just looking for something simple, and I got the most complicated relationship there is."

"You'll find the right guy eventually. It'll take some time, but it'll happen." He grabbed his beer off the table and took a drink.

"How's the job hunt going?"

"I applied to a few places in downtown Seattle. Haven't heard back yet. But honestly, not being employed is pretty nice."

Finn leaned forward on his knees, his gaze focused on the game. "You mean, being a freeloader is nice."

"Hey, you were a freeloader at my place," Colton replied.

"Was I?" Finn challenged. "I did all the laundry, the dishes, and the cooking. What did you do?"

"I put a roof over your head." Colton argued with his brother all the time, but they were undeniably close. There was a sense of camaraderie between them that you could feel.

Finn shook his head slightly. "I've put a nicer roof over your head."

"Whoa, that was a nice apartment." Now Colton wasn't watching the game at all and only looked at his brother. "It had a big living room and a decent kitchen. I loved that apartment... I miss that apartment."

"Someone already moved in," I said. "A young guy who just got divorced."

"Really?" Colton asked. "Gay or straight?"

He'd seemed straight to me. "Straight."

"Damn." Colton stared at his beer. "But on the other hand, he could be perfect for you. You're both newly divorced and not looking for anything serious."

"With the guy who lives across the hall from me?" I asked incredulously. "That wouldn't get weird..."

"Is he hot?" Colton asked bluntly.

I was aware of Finn in the room, of his eyes on my side profile. The guilt made me mask my true thoughts. I had no reason to feel guilty for being attracted to a man. Finn and I would never be together, so it didn't matter. Come to think of it, I'd never heard him compliment a woman before. Even when the sexy cheerleaders danced on TV, he never made a comment. "He's not bad to look at..."

"Maybe something will happen there," Colton said.

I looked at the time and realized I should get home. I had a long day at work tomorrow, especially since I had to count all the inventory. It was the thing I hated most about my job. "It's getting late, so I should get going."

"I would say the same thing, but I don't have to work tomorrow." Colton grinned.

I gave him a playful smack on the arm before I rose to my feet. "Jerk." I grabbed my phone and prepared to request an Uber.

Finn got off the couch. "I'll drive you."

"No, it's okay. I'll just do an Uber." The game was on, and it was getting late. I didn't want Finn to do anything more for me than he already had.

He grabbed a sweater off the back of the chair and zipped it up. "I said I'll drive you."

"You should finish the game."

He turned back to me, his dark blue sweater fitting his muscular shoulders perfectly. "I said I'll drive you." The warning in his tone told me not to question him again.

Colton leaned back in the couch. "He can be a little much, huh?"

Finn ignored his brother then walked into the garage where his truck was waiting. It was a large vehicle for a man who just drove to work at the hospital. He opened the garage then unlocked the doors with the press of a button.

We climbed in and drove away.

It was dark outside, especially since the roads were dimly lit. As we drove closer to the city, the roads were illuminated better. The signs from the shops and businesses came into focus. Light sprinkles of rain started to hit the front window.

It seemed like it rained every day.

I looked out the passenger window and tried to ignore the rising heat between us. Any time we were alone together when there was no chance of anyone seeing us together, I always sensed this adrenaline in my veins. My neck felt hot, and my lips felt anxious. My new neighbor was handsome, but he didn't send chills down my spine the way Finn did. "I appreciate you driving me home, but you really didn't have to do that."

He drove with one hand on the wheel, his eyes on the road. "After everything you've done for me, it's the least I can do."

"What have I done for you?" I asked, being serious.

"You picked out all my furniture. You're going shopping with me on Thursday."

"That's just what friends do."

"So, that's what I am to you?" he asked, his profile slightly visible from the lights of his dashboard. The shadow on his jaw made him sexier, made him darker. The ink from his tattoos peeked out from underneath the sleeves of his sweater. "A friend?"

"Yes. I would hope the same from you."

He made a left turn, and his eyes shifted back and forth as he scanned the road ahead of him. He made it into the city then pulled up in front of the apartment building.

"Well, thank you—"

"I'll walk you to the door."

"You don't need to—"

He gave me a fierce look that shut me up right away.

I hopped out of the truck, and we walked into the

building together. We took the stairs to my floor and moved down the hallway to my door.

He walked beside me, his arms stiff at his sides as he kept a few feet between us.

My throat was noticeably dry because the tension sucked all the moisture out of the air. I hated being alone with this man because it did terrible things to my cardiovascular system. I always felt like I was on the verge of a heart attack.

We reached my door, and I pulled my keys out of my clutch.

He stood near the door, like he wasn't going anywhere until I was actually across the threshold.

I got the door open then looked at him. "Thanks for dinner."

"You mean pizza and beer?" he teased.

"That's my favorite kind of dinner."

He continued to linger, like this conversation was far from over.

I stared into his pretty blue eyes and imagined his body on top of mine, his dog tags dragging along my chest as he moved. I pictured my fingertips feeling those rocks for abs again, sliding against the sweat that trickled everywhere. My body wanted to be full of him, to feel our lips locked together with a mixture of kisses and hot breaths. Maybe I couldn't be around this man, after all. "Goodnight, Finn."

"Goodnight, baby." Before I could get inside, his

thick arm wrapped around my body, and he pulled me in for a hug.

The second his hand moved underneath my shirt and felt my bare skin, I lost all reason to resist. I moved into his chest and felt his body surround me. If testosterone had a scent, it was the scent of Finn. My forehead moved against his chest, and I closed my eyes, accepting a moment of weakness.

His other arm wrapped around me, and he rested his chin on the top of my head.

I closed my eyes as I enjoyed his powerful body wrapped around mine. Someone could interpret the gesture as friendly affection, but I felt practically naked and covered in sweat. My breathing was deep and labored, but I also felt comfortable enough to fall asleep in his arms. I wanted to stay like this forever, to feel his scent envelop me.

He held me on the doorstep for a long time, his arms as strong as iron gates. Unless he released me, I would have no chance of escape.

He suddenly released me, my body turning cold the second his affection ceased. Without saying a word, he turned around and walked away. His heavy footsteps receded down the hallway, and his muscular back was perfectly upright with his powerful posture.

I watched him until he was gone from my sight. Then I stepped inside my empty apartment.

And wished he were still there.

2

COLTON

W hen I woke up the next day, Finn was sitting at the kitchen table with all the windows open. It was a clear day, so while it was beautiful, it was ten degrees colder than usual. His living room had tons of windows that showed the large backyard. He sat with the newspaper beside him, his laptop open, and his notes in front of him.

I made a cup of coffee then joined him. "You always have a ton of paperwork."

"Because I see a lot of patients."

"How many patients do you see in twelve hours?"

"Twenty-four to thirty."

"Really?" I asked in surprise. "That's over two an hour."

He kept his eyes on the paper. "I told you I was fast."

"You make me feel lazy."

"Because you are lazy."

I rolled my eyes. "I haven't talked to Aaron in a while. I would go out and try to meet someone, but saying I'm unemployed isn't sexy."

"But if you tell them you're a lawyer between jobs, that is sexy."

"Not as sexy as being a doctor."

He kept his eyes on the paper. "I could get laid even if I weren't a doctor."

"Because you're built like a brick house."

"Not true. I'm ripped. There's a difference."

I rolled my eyes again even though he wasn't looking at me. "I hate you sometimes."

"I hate you all the time." He shut the paper and placed it to the side.

"Any problems with Pepper?"

He finally looked up and met my gaze. "Meaning?"

"When you took her home last night."

His eyes dilated slightly. "No. I walked her to her door and left."

"You walked her to her door?" I asked incredulously.

"What's wrong with that?"

"Just seems excessive..." I noticed the way my brother went out of his way for her. He actually behaved like a gentleman anytime it concerned her. Would he have offered to take home Zach or anyone else?

"I respect her. That doesn't happen very often."

Maybe he respected her because she was my wife... I mean, ex-wife. She still had my last name, so we were still family.

"Would you rather I treat her like garbage?"

"No. I just—"

"Then let it go." He turned back to his computer.

I didn't broach the subject again, knowing I was just being paranoid. "Have you talked to Mom?"

"Only every day."

"Has she said anything...?"

"No. But she'll come around."

"You really think so?"

"I know so, Colt." He typed on his computer. "I know you don't have a job, but I do. So quiet down so I can get these dictations done. I have to work in a few hours."

Not having a job was nice, but I noticed how bored I was. My brother worked forty hours a week, and when he was home, he still had to work a few hours every day. He didn't always have time to play ball in the driveway. Then he spent his extra time at the gym or picking up groceries. The guy was busy. "I'm gonna visit Pepper, then. I'll see you later."

I WALKED into the lingerie shop and spotted her behind the counter. She was making notes on her clipboard, and judging by the large box beside her, she was checking all her inventory. There wasn't a single customer inside.

"Slow day?"

She looked up at the sound of my voice. "Customers don't usually come in until after lunch. I use the morning to catch up on paperwork. Unless you want to buy something?" She grinned.

"You got anything in black?" I walked up to the counter and rested my elbows on the surface.

She chuckled. "I've got everything in black."

"It's always been my color..."

She turned back to her notes. "So what brings you here?"

"Finn is busy, and I'm bored."

"You could get a job..."

"I'm trying."

"But you could be trying now."

"I am a lot pickier about the offices I want to work in now. I'd rather be in an environment I really want to be in instead of just taking anything."

"That's smart."

"But that means there's a lot more waiting around. Finn works all those shifts, and then he has to do paperwork when he's home. I was hoping we could play basketball all day, but he's got too much shit going on."

"He's a hard worker."

I rolled my eyes. "Or a party pooper."

"I know you don't really think that about him."

I respected my brother immensely, even if I never mentioned it. "So, learn anything about your new neighbor?"

"I haven't seen him since the other day."

"And how hot is he?"

She shrugged. "Pretty hot. He came home in his gym clothes, and he definitely has a nice body."

"Why did he get divorced?"

She gave me a glare. "You think I'm really going to ask that in the middle of the hallway?"

I shrugged. "You told him you're divorced too."

"And I wouldn't want him to ask why. Maybe if I get to know him, it'll come up."

"Maybe we should hang out at your place and see if we can learn anything more. We still haven't settled if he's gay or straight."

"I'm pretty sure he's straight."

"Why?" I asked.

"He stared at me a lot."

"Ooh...maybe you have a rebound." Now that Pepper had had a relationship with Jax that failed, I wasn't uncomfortable with her seeing other guys. It was starting to feel normal, like we really were friends who talked about getting laid like everyone else. I was slowly letting go of the fact that she was my ex-wife. She still felt like family, but in a friendly way.

"The last time I had a rebound, it ended up being a nightmare…"

"Only because one night with you just isn't enough."

She gave a slight smile.

"And since this guy is divorced, you probably have a lot in common."

"That's true…"

"So maybe he's perfect for you."

"I hope the criteria to be perfect for me is more than just being divorced. I have interests and hobbies like everyone else."

"Tell him you own a lingerie shop." I snapped my fingers. "That'll be perfect."

"But he lives across the hall from me. Wouldn't that be weird?"

I shrugged. "If it's just a fuck-buddy situation, why would it be?"

"I don't know. I've never hooked up with a neighbor before."

"Well, there's a first time for everything. What time of day did you see him last time?"

"After work."

"Perfect. We'll linger in the hallway until he comes home from the gym."

Pepper shook her head slightly, like the suggestion was ridiculous. "Acting like a desperate idiot isn't my style. I may be desperate right now, but not that desperate."

"How else are we supposed to run into him?" I asked. "We only have the short window of when he walks from the stairs to his front door. Desperate measures are required. Unless you know where he works or what gym he goes to."

She shook her head. "I'm not desperate enough to ask. How about this? We go to my place to watch the game like normal people—and not spy on the guy across the hall."

I was eager for Pepper to find the right guy so she could have the relationship she deserved. The day she got married would hurt me, would make me remember how happy we were together, but it would also comfort me. She deserved everything I'd failed to give her. "That's not as adventurous, but fine. We'll pick up some beer on the way."

"That sounds much better."

"You can invite Finn over if you want." She had to wrap a towel around the cap of the bottle before she twisted it off. She tossed the cloth and cap on the coffee table before she took a drink.

"He's working today."

"Oh, that's right." She pulled her knees to her chest and watched the game, paying attention to the plays and the score because she was genuinely interested.

"My brother really likes you."

She almost spat out her beer as she said, "What? What do you mean?"

I eyed the drops of liquid that stained the front of her blouse. "He told me he walked you all the way to your front door last night. That's not like Finn. He's not the kind of man that practices chivalry."

She wiped her mouth with the back of her forearm. "I think he's kinder than you give him credit for."

"No, he just likes you. He told me he respects you—and that's hard to accomplish."

She kept her eyes on the TV.

"What is it with you and my family?" I asked. "Every single one of them is obsessed with you."

She shrugged. "I don't know. I guess we just click..."

"Too bad they didn't get you instead of me in the divorce."

She tapped my arm lightly. "Don't do that. You know it's not true."

"Eh...it's partially true." I clinked my bottle against hers. "But that's okay. I fell in love with you the first night we met. It doesn't surprise me that you have that effect on everyone else."

She turned quiet as she watched the TV.

"You want to go bowling on Thursday night?" Zach and I were thinking of getting a team together to make it a weekly thing.

"I would, but I already have plans."

"What are you doing?"

"Finn and I are going shopping for his kitchen stuff at Williams-Sonoma."

"Are you charging him for all these services?" I asked incredulously.

"No," she said with a chuckle. "That's what friends do."

"You don't have to help him, you know. It's nice of you and everything, but you don't need to bend over backward for him."

"I really don't mind. I know Finn started off as just your brother...but he's become a part of my life too. Besides, he's a veteran. After everything he's done for our country, you bet your ass I'm gonna help him with whatever he needs."

I nodded in agreement. "That's a good point."

A knock sounded on the door.

"Expecting anyone?" I asked.

"No." She set her beer down then went to the door. After looking through the peephole, she turned to me. She mouthed, "It's him!"

"Who?" I mouthed back, rising to my feet.

She thrust her finger in the direction across the hall. "Hot neighbor."

I jumped to my feet. "I'll hide in the bathroom so you can have sex on the couch."

She gave me an incredulous look. "What? No, just sit down." She pointed at the couch.

I lowered myself back down.

She flipped her hair over her shoulder then opened the door. "Hey, Damon. How are you?"

He was dressed in jeans and a t-shirt, and Pepper was right, he did have a nice body. I smiled widely and tried to act natural, but my jaw hurt from grinning so big, and I felt out of place just staring at him.

Damon glanced at me and gave an awkward look of acknowledgment. "Good. I just wanted to see if you wanted to watch the game, but you're obviously on a date—"

"I'm not her date," I blurted. "Just her gay bestie."

Pepper turned to me, silently telling me to play it cool. She turned back to Damon. "We were watching the game too. Would you like to join us?"

Now that he knew I was gay, he didn't seem so uncomfortable. "Sure." He stepped inside then extended his hand to shake mine. "Damon. Nice to meet you."

"Colton. You want a beer?"

"Sure."

I grabbed one from the fridge and handed it over.

Pepper sat in between us, seeming cool and composed, but I could tell she was nervous. "Seahawk fan?"

"Would I be alive right now if I weren't?" Damon asked with a chuckle.

"Good point." She held her beer on her thigh and kept her eyes on the TV. "Did you just get off work?"

"Yep. I have a nine-to-five." He relaxed into the couch and rested his ankle on the opposite knee.

"What do you do?" she asked.

"I'm an accountant," he answered. "What about you?"

"I own a boutique clothing store in town." She purposely left the best part out.

"It's a lingerie store," I added, knowing it would make her look better, not worse.

Pepper shot me a glare.

"A lingerie store?" Damon asked. "Wow...that's pretty cool."

I shot her a triumphant look back.

The conversation shifted to sports, a subject I couldn't contribute much to. They talked back and forth, everything lighthearted and easy. The guy was easygoing and laid-back, and most importantly, he was super-hot. His body was impossible to mask under his clothing, and I could tell he was all muscle, soft skin, and the perfect amount of hair.

Too bad he was straight.

I wanted to give Pepper the best chance of success, so I made an excuse for leaving. "I have to pick up Zach from the airport. I'll talk to you later."

Pepper didn't question the lie.

"Nice to meet you, Damon." I gave him a thumbs-up before I walked out.

When I shut the door, I felt a slight twinge of jealousy. It was only a matter of time before Pepper fell in love with a new man and started her own life. It was a tough transition, but one that needed to happen. Because I cared about her happiness much more than my own.

Finn walked through the door an hour before midnight. In his dark blue scrubs with a deep cut down the front, hints of his ink were visible. It was a short-sleeved top, so his arms were decorated with the black tattoos that covered up almost every patch of skin. He set his satchel on the dining table then moved to the fridge.

"Since you drink so much, how do you manage not to do it at work?" I sat on the couch with the TV on.

He pulled out the box of leftover pizza and ate a few slices at the counter. "I'm too busy to think about booze."

I noticed that he hadn't brought a woman home in a couple of weeks. He used to have someone over at least three times a week, and now that he was living in his own home, I'd expected him to be more promiscuous. "Haven't met any lady friends lately?"

He looked up from the box and eyed me, his black stethoscope hanging around his neck. "What's that supposed to mean?"

"You usually bring women home, but you haven't in a while."

He took another bite and didn't answer my question. "What'd you do today?"

"Hung out with Pepper."

"Poor girl."

I glared at the guy. "Don't feel sorry for her. That new roommate across the hall came over to watch the game. And this guy is sexy. You can tell he hits the gym every day, and he has dimples in his cheeks every time he smiles. He's cute."

Finn stopped chewing, his eyes narrowing on my face.

"What? I'm gay. What do you expect me to say?"

"Does she like this guy?"

I shrugged. "She doesn't know him very well. But he's super-sexy, so what's there not to like? They're both recently divorced, so they have a lot in common. At least, I assume they'll have a lot in common once they start talking. When I was over there, all they cared about was the game. I bailed to give them some privacy."

Finn shut the box and shoved it into the fridge. Then he left his stuff behind on the table and headed to the stairs.

"How was work?"

He kept going, like he hadn't heard a word I said.

"Finn?"

He reached the top of the stairs and kept going.

"Geez...he's moody."

3

PEPPER

"Well, that wasn't much of a game..." I turned down the volume on the remote. "Thirteen to three...snooze fest."

He chuckled and set his empty bottle on the coffee table. "Yeah. But the beauty of football is that it's on two days a week, sometimes three."

"Very true."

"Well, thanks for having me over." He didn't rise to his feet and head to the door. He stayed on his end of the couch, subtly glancing at me from time to time.

"Yeah, of course."

Silence stretched for a while, like he had something to say but couldn't spit it out. "I'd like to ask you out, but I don't think I'm ready for that. It's just too soon, you know? Now that my ex is taking things slow..." He shook his head, exhaling in bitterness.

"Nasty divorce?"

"A bit. But she cheated, so I think I had every right to be nasty."

"Oh...I'm sorry. How long were you married?"

"Three years."

"That's ironic. Same with me."

"I hope your husband didn't cheat. He'd be stupid to cheat on a woman as beautiful as you."

I couldn't stop myself from making a sarcastic laugh. "Look at you. She's definitely stupid."

He shrugged. "She blindsided me. I didn't see it coming. I thought everything was fine..."

"That seems to be how it happens. Same with me."

"And then I caught her sucking my best friend's dick at the foot of our bed." He shook his head. "I put him in the hospital, and I scared the shit out of her."

"Damn...a double betrayal."

"Yeah...so I'm gonna be messed up for a while."

"And you have every right to be. I'm not looking for a relationship right now either. I've been divorced for almost a year now, but the idea of jumping into a new relationship doesn't sound appealing. I was seeing this guy for a while, wanting something purely physical, but he kept wanting something more...and it blew up in my face."

He turned to me, his green eyes focused on my face. "May I ask why your marriage ended?"

I had to get used to telling people. I shouldn't feel ashamed about it. "He realized he was gay."

"Ooh...that's rough."

"It was actually Colton. We're really good friends and still have a strong relationship. It took a while to get there, but it happened."

"Wow...that must have been hard."

"In the beginning. But like I said, it gets better. I promise."

"I'll hold on to that." He finished the last of his beer before he looked at me. "I'm not looking for a lay or a girlfriend right now. But I am looking for a friend. Maybe we can hang out? I might post a few pictures of us on my social media accounts just to make my ex jealous...but that's the extent of it."

I laughed at his humor. "Yeah, that would be nice. I love sports, bowling, and of course, eating."

"What a coincidence, I love eating too. It looks like we're going to get along pretty well."

ON THURSDAY EVENING, I opened the door and came face-to-face with Finn. It was a cold evening, so he wore a dark blue jacket over his gray V-neck. Most of his ink was covered, with the exception of a few images that stretched across his chest toward his neck. He looked at me in greeting, like that was more sufficient than saying a few words.

He'd insisted on picking me up, so I locked the door behind me, and we walked off together. We made it to his truck, got inside, and then drove to the mall where the store was located.

"How was work?" I asked, breaking the tense silence with small talk. Sometimes when I was around Finn, it seemed like he hated me. Other times, it seemed like he couldn't live without me. There was no in-between with this man. It was just one extreme to the next.

"Fine." He pulled into a parking spot and killed the engine. "It was busy. I had to stay an hour late because there were so many patients."

"That's nice of you."

"Sometimes we have to put in extra work for the greater good. Otherwise, those patients would keep waiting, and then new patients would be waiting longer. It would turn into a crisis."

"It's good that you see the big picture."

"The unfortunate truth is we don't have enough doctors, so the ones who are working have to compensate."

"I didn't know that."

We left the truck and walked into the store. He

barely looked around before he turned to me. "Work your magic, baby."

When he'd first called me by that nickname, it was rough on the skin and intimate on the heart. But now, he'd been calling me that for so long that I was used to it. I couldn't imagine him calling me by my actual name.

I looked at the different plate options and ignored the ones I liked, the classy ones with red roses printed on the rim. His kitchen was dark colors with granite countertops. I looked through the selection until I found a plate collection in the most beautiful hue of gray. "What about this?"

"You're the expert here." He stood beside me, smelling like a hot shower.

"But do you like it?"

"I like anything as long as I can eat off it."

When he was this close to me, I felt my hair stand on end. His scent entered my nose, and I was aware of how close we were to each other, like an engaged couple registering for their special day. "Well, that was easy."

"I'm not a picky guy."

"I've noticed..." I moved to the silverware next and looked through the selections before I found something that would match. I felt his blue eyes drill into my body, that scorching sensation as all-consuming as fire. I looked up and met his look.

He didn't look away. He held the intimate expression like he wasn't the least bit scared to share his intensity with me. He didn't care if anyone else was watching. He didn't care whether it made me comfortable or uncomfortable.

This friendship was becoming more strained by the day.

I cleared my throat. "What do you think of these?" I turned my gaze to the utensils, needing to break the connection first.

"Whatever you want, baby." He drifted away and headed to the appliance section, like he knew I needed space after the way he'd suffocated me with his gaze. That man was the most intense person on the planet. He could be equally threatening and comforting at the same time.

I picked out a few other things, and when I went to join him, I saw a pretty woman talking to him in front of the toasters. She wore a low-cut top, fuck-me heels, and bright red lipstick that every guy imagined smeared across his cock. Jealousy raged through me at the way she stood so close to him, at the way she was clearly hitting on him.

But I had no right to feel anything.

This man wasn't mine. He would never be mine.

He would always be my ex's brother.

So I turned away and gave him privacy. I went to

look at the blenders, even though I'd never seen him make smoothies.

A few minutes later, he appeared at my side. "I never use blenders."

"What about a food processor?"

"No." His eyes moved along the shelf of selections. "All I have left that I need is a knife set."

"Well, I'm not the best choice for picking out stuff like that, so you might be a better fit."

He walked over to the large knives that were used for heavy-duty cutting. He examined them with his hands in his pockets, his eyes roaming over the different descriptions.

"Got a date for tonight?" I couldn't stop myself from asking the question, from letting my jealousy dictate my actions. I wished I could take it back the second I spat those words out.

"She's not my type."

I raised an eyebrow. "First Stella and now this girl... Beautiful women aren't your type? You just said you weren't picky."

"I'm not picky."

"Then why aren't you going to go out with her?"

He turned to me, his eyes cold like frost on the lawn first thing in the morning. "Because I don't want to. That's why." He slightly pivoted his body so we were face-to-face. He bent his neck so he could bring his face closer to mine, let those blue eyes eat me alive. He held the stance for a long time, not backing down despite the heat rising between us.

I swallowed the lump in my throat and felt the air leave my lungs. I'd pressured him about this woman because I didn't want him to see her—and he knew that. Our feelings were so obvious to each other that it felt idiotic to pretend otherwise. I wanted this man to be my friend, but that was impossible. My fingers ached to dig into his hair, to feel that powerful body and tug it closer to mine. I wanted to kiss him and never stop, be naked and sweaty. I didn't just want this man for a night, a night of good sex and endless orgasms. I wanted him just to have him, to feel his strong heartbeat against mine.

He was the first to pull away. "I'll get this set. Let's go."

THE BACK of his truck was loaded with everything he'd bought, and the drive home back to my apartment was long, quiet, and awkward. The radio wasn't even on so we just sat in silence.

Why did I have to say anything? Why couldn't I keep my stupid mouth shut?

Why did I have to care about this man at all?

Every day I had to remind myself who he was—my ex-husband's brother.

If there was any man in the world who was off-limits—it was him.

But it didn't change the way I felt. It didn't eliminate the gnawing feeling in my gut.

I looked out the window and watched my apartment come into view. He parked the truck then killed the engine.

"With all your stuff in the back, it's probably better if you don't walk me to my door."

He stared at me with that same look of annoyance. "All that shit can be replaced. You can't." He got out of the truck.

Why did he have to say things like that? Things that made me want him more. I got out of the truck and walked up the stairs to my floor. We headed to my door just as Damon stepped out of his apartment, dressed in jeans and a t-shirt like he was about to go out.

Damon's eyes lit up once he saw me. "It's my favorite neighbor. What are you up to?"

"My friend just got a new house, so we went shopping for the essentials."

Finn looked at me, like he didn't appreciate the way I'd introduced him.

"Sorry, this is Finn. Finn, this is my new neighbor, Damon."

Damon shook his hand. "Nice to meet you. I'm sure your new place is going to look great."

All Finn did was nod in response.

"He's actually Colton's older brother," I explained, even though that information wasn't relevant.

"Oh, so brother-in-law," Damon said. "I mean, former brother-in-law."

I never thought of Finn with that title, but it was the truth. He was my brother by marriage at one point —and I wanted to sleep with him. "Where are you off to?"

"Going to a friend's place," he said. "But maybe we should get together for the game this weekend."

"Yeah, that would be cool."

Damon waved before he walked off. "I'll catch you later, then." He walked away.

Finn turned around and watched him go until he was out of sight.

Now the tension increased tenfold.

I'd just gotten upset when I saw a beautiful woman try to take him home. He probably didn't like my new handsome neighbor, a man who had access to me any time he wanted. I spotted the anger in his eyes, so I felt the compulsion to say something. "We're just friends..."

Finn stared at me long and hard, never blinking.

"He just got divorced, so he's not looking for anything right now."

"And you asked?"

"No," I said quickly. "He said he wanted to ask me

out but wasn't ready for it. I told him I wasn't ready for anything either." Even though I was totally ready for this if it were a possibility. The past wouldn't seem relevant at all, and I would invite this man to my bed—and beg him to stay forever. "So we decided to be friends... since we have a lot in common."

Finn kept up his stare.

I didn't owe this man an explanation, but I felt the need to explain I wasn't seeing anyone, that I didn't just break up with Jax and was then jumping into bed with some other guy. Not that it mattered...but it mattered to me.

The only way I could stop that stare was if I turned away. I grabbed my key and unlocked the door just so I could do that, get this man's eyes off me. Once I faced the door, I released the air I was holding in my lungs. The door swung inward then I turned back around. "Well...goodnight." Were we going to have another embrace on the doorstep, affection that belonged between lovers rather than friends?

He stepped closer to me then leaned his head down until our foreheads were touching. His arms didn't circle me like last time. Instead, he just stood in front of me, our heads close together. "Goodnight, baby."

This was definitely not friendly. This was definitely not platonic. What existed between us was so hot and fiery that my internal temperature was always a hundred and twenty degrees. Instead of things getting easier, they just got harder. "Finn...this has to stop." I didn't want to be the kind of person that betrayed my best friend. I didn't want to be the woman who came between two brothers. I wanted to be the loyal and honest person I'd been my whole life. But when temptation stared me in the face like this, I struggled to resist.

His hand slid into the back of my hair, and he tilted my chin up to meet his gaze. "I haven't kissed you. I haven't invited you to bed." His hand cupped my cheek as he looked into my gaze, his blue eyes mesmerizing.

"But this is worse...because all I want to do is kiss you and go to bed."

He closed his eyes for a moment, the words making him throb. "I control the things I can. But I can't control the way I feel. I won't apologize for it." He pressed his lips to my forehead and kissed me before he stepped away. He didn't look at me again before he walked off, leaving me standing still and treasuring that innocent kiss.

I APPROACHED the table and found Colton's mother sitting there, dressed in a blue blazer with a white top underneath. Her shoulder-length hair was perfectly styled, like she'd just gone to the beauty parlor that afternoon.

She rose to greet me and enveloped me in a motherly hug. "Hey, sweetheart. You look wonderful."

"Thank you." I hugged her back, loving her the way a girl would love her mother. I didn't appreciate the way she'd behaved weeks ago, but she'd always been so kind to me that her tantrum didn't change my opinion of her.

We sat down, ordered drinks and appetizers, and then started talking about the biggest event in our lives.

"I wish I'd known you two were getting a divorce, sweetheart. I would have been there for you."

"I know...it was really hard in the beginning. After we signed our divorce papers, it took me three months away from Colton to finally be at peace again. I was hurt and angry with him for a while."

"As you had every right to be." It was amazing how she spoke to me as a mother, as if Colton weren't actually her son. She could love both of us equally and separately. "This has been so difficult for us. It doesn't matter to us if Colton is gay, straight, or a giraffe, but losing you is just unbearable. I should have known you were too good to be true."

"Well, you'll never lose me. Colton and I are still best friends, and I'll always be around."

"Until you get married and start a family of your own—and that's perfectly okay."

"Wouldn't my husband be part of the family too?" I asked. "I could never marry someone who didn't accept my relationship with Colton. That's a requirement to be in a relationship with me."

"That's sweet." She smiled at me.

"And Colton will get married someday. I won't be your daughter-in-law, but you will have another son. And I'm sure he'll be great."

"Yes...eventually. Right now, all I can think about is what we're losing, not what we'll gain in the future."

I tried to be understanding because all of this was new to her. Colton and I had had almost a full year to get used to the changes in our lives, but she'd only had a few weeks. "Are you going to talk to Colton soon? He's still upset about the way you left things."

"Yes, of course." She sipped her iced tea. "It's just been hard. I didn't mean to blow up at him the way I did. I was just so upset by the way you were hurt in all of this. You're a daughter to me, and I'm protective of you."

"I know..."

"That must have been so hard for you. And if he had any notion that he felt that way, he should have told you. He shouldn't have waited until all this time had passed. It's unacceptable."

"It hurt in the beginning, but I'm in a good place

now. Honestly, I wouldn't trade our time together for anything, so you don't need to be angry with him."

Her eyes softened. "See? This is why I love you so much. You're so good, you know? Such a kind heart that sees the best in people."

"I see the best in Colton because that's all there is to see. You really should talk to him soon. He's hurting and needs love and acceptance right now."

"You're right... I'll call him tonight." Her phone rested on the surface next to her drink, so the screen was visible when it lit up with a phone call. It vibrated on the table and made a loud clanking noise.

I spotted the name on the screen.

Finn.

"Sorry, sweetheart. I need to take this." She took the call and held it to her ear. "Hey, honey."

I could hear Finn's voice over the line, deep and masculine. "Sorry I didn't call you back yesterday. I was stuck at the hospital for an extra three hours. Had three ambulances come in at the same time, and we were understaffed."

Why did this man have to be so sexy? His voice was naturally seductive, and he was a hero every single day of his life. He was incredible. And hearing him speak to his mother with such respect was a turn-on too.

"Oh, don't worry about it," she said. "I can only imagine how hectic it can get. What are you doing now?"

"Just stopped by the store. Ran out of laundry detergent."

"You know I can do your laundry whenever you need, honey."

Finn chuckled over the line. "I know, Mom. But you did my laundry for eighteen years. You've paid your dues."

I didn't want to sit there and listen to this.

"I'm actually having lunch with Pepper right now. We're at the Cheesecake Factory. Would you like to join us?"

No.

"I'm just a few stores down from you. That's ironic."

"Is that a yes?" she asked excitedly.

"Sure."

"Alright, I'll see you soon." She hung up then looked at me. "You don't mind if Finn joins us, right?"

Yes, I did mind. "Of course not."

"Great. I saw him so little during his ten years in the military that I try to soak up every moment I have with him. When he first enlisted, I was so crushed. Watching your little boy go off to war like that...it's the worst feeling in the world. But when I see who he's become, I feel so proud."

"You should be proud." He was the most honorable man I'd ever met. He was a war hero, and not once did he brag about it. He was always respectful of everyone around him, but he wasn't afraid to put someone in their place when they deserved it. He was protective of the people he cared about. He really was the perfect man.

"I am," she said. "It's too bad you never really got to know him until recently. He missed your wedding and all the holidays…"

"I've gotten to know him since he got here, and I admire him. He's such a contrast to Colton."

"Yes, they are very different."

Finn walked inside a moment later, wearing jeans and a tight t-shirt. Every woman in the bar turned his way the second he made his presence known. Eyes grazed over his muscular arms and his tall height. The man was so ripped that I wondered if he was unhealthy for having such little body fat. He spotted us, and his eyes settled on me.

Even with his mother in the same room, he looked at me the way he always did.

Like I was his.

His mother rose and hugged him. "Honey, I'm so happy to see you." She hugged him tightly, just the way a mother hugged her son on the first day of kindergarten.

He allowed her to squeeze him as much as she wanted. He patted her on the back gently, not embarrassed by his mother's affection. "I'm happy to see you too, Mom." When he pulled away, he righted her chair for her and helped her sit down.

I'd never seen him pull out the chair for anyone, not even me.

This man was killing me.

He came around the table and took the seat beside me.

I could smell his scent the second he was near, feel his masculine presence flood my veins. My heart started to slam into the walls of my chest as my nerve endings fired off in excitement. His arm brushed against mine as he got comfortable.

I hoped it wasn't obvious to his mother how attracted I was to her son.

He turned to me, and it was one of the few times he addressed me by my name. "Hey, Pepper."

It felt weird not hearing him call me baby. I definitely preferred the nickname over my actual name—at least on his lips. "Hey..."

"Pepper and I were just talking about Colton," his mother said. "I'll give him a call tonight to smooth things over. I just needed some time to adjust to everything. Losing Pepper is the hardest part of all this. I want her to move on and be happy with a new man... but I don't want to let her go either."

Finn grabbed his menu and looked at the options as he spoke. "I don't want to let her go either."

4

COLTON

I kept staring at Finn on the other couch.

Because he actually had a shirt on.

Since the day we'd moved in together, that had not happened. Regardless of the weather or the company, he always chose to go shirtless. Seeing him fully clothed was just weird. "What's with the shirt?"

He kept his eyes on the TV.

The doorbell rang.

"That's why." He turned off the screen then rose to his feet. "You have a date coming over?"

"If I had a date, my shirt would definitely be off." He walked to the front door then returned with my mother in tow.

"Mom?" I rose to my feet, surprised to see her show up unannounced.

Finn stepped away. "I'll be in my room..."

I stared at my mom in surprise, shocked she would stop by without calling first. Judging by the remorse in her eyes, she was there to make amends.

I was relieved that this was finally over, that she would be my mom again. "Hey…"

She came into the living room and took a seat. "I've been doing a lot of thinking lately, and I want to apologize for the way I reacted. Your father is sorry too. It was so much information to process at one time, and I just couldn't handle it."

"I know, Mom."

She patted my thigh. "We couldn't care less about who you love or who you want to be with. It doesn't make a difference to us at all. Do whatever makes you happy. Life is so short, so be honest to yourself."

"Thanks…" I wish she'd said this weeks ago, but late was better than never.

"Losing Pepper was so hard for me. I always worried one of you boys would marry a psycho girl… and then you brought home Pepper. She's lovely. Absolutely perfect. She's such a part of our family that I can't picture life without her."

"Maybe we can get Finn to marry her, then. Keep her in the family."

She chuckled. "Not the worst idea I've ever heard." She looked around the living room before she turned back to me. "This is the first time I've seen his new place. It's very nice. I find it hard to believe that he picked out everything."

"Pepper did, actually."

"See what I mean?" she said with a chuckle.

"But we aren't going to lose her, Mom. She'll always be in my life. We love each other too much to let go."

She smiled, but it was in a painful way. "I know. It just won't be the same when she remarries."

I nodded slightly. "Yeah, I guess. But she won't disappear either."

"True. I was so upset when I imagined you hurting that wonderful woman. She's already been through so much. We're the only real family she's ever had."

"And we'll always be her family," I said. "No matter what."

She patted my thigh again. "So...do you forgive me?"

I rolled my eyes. "Of course, Mom."

"Great. So...are you seeing anyone?"

"You really want to talk about this?" I asked incredulously. "You hardly asked that when I was straight."

"Well, you were with Pepper for five years. That's a big chunk of time when I didn't have to ask. So...?"

"I've been kinda talking to this guy named Aaron, but I don't think it's going to go anywhere. I need to put myself out there more, but it's been difficult. I've been a little intimidated by everything."

"You have a lot to offer, son. Nothing to be intimidated by."

I smiled, relieved I had my mother back. "Thanks..."

She patted my arm. "Finn tells me you moved in because you quit your job. Have you found anything else?"

"I actually have a job interview tomorrow. It's for an environmental group. I hope I get it because it's something I'm really interested in. It's been a while since I've had an interview, so hopefully I make a good impression."

"You will. Just be yourself."

"I wish I could be Finn. He could walk in and nail any interview—without being a lawyer."

"That's because he's confident. Just be a little more self-assured. People notice those things."

And all the women noticed Finn's particularly attractive traits.

"I had lunch with Pepper yesterday."

"You did?" I asked in surprise. She never mentioned it to me.

"Yeah, it was nice to catch up. She assured me that she'll always be in our lives and that she was in a good place. Colton, you're very lucky to have a woman like that love you. She's so loyal to you. That's rare."

If I had been married to someone else, my divorce would have been completely different. I couldn't imagine anyone else being so compassionate and understanding. But Pepper treated the situation self-lessly, caring about me instead of her. "I know...she's the perfect woman. I just hope she finds the perfect guy."

"She will, honey. All in good time."

I WALKED in the front door, spotted my brother at the kitchen table, and did a terrible version of the moon-walk across the hardwood floor.

Finn watched me, a slightly bored look on his face. "I'm guessing the interview went well."

"Yes." I did a spin in place then gave him two thumbs-up. "So good, they hired me on the spot."

"That's awesome, man." He smiled slightly, as wide of a smile as a man like him could make. "I told you everything would fall into place. So, when are you moving out?"

I gave him an angry look. "That's all you care about?"

"I said congratulations, and I meant it. But yes, I care about you moving out."

"I don't get my first paycheck for a couple of weeks, and I've been blowing through my savings like crazy."

"On what?" he asked. "Because you don't pay rent or utilities here."

"When I had to spend double on utilities and food when I had a roommate…"

His eyes softened when I made the comeback. "Fine. You can stay a little longer."

"I wish I could get my old apartment back. I wonder if that hunk wants a roommate."

"I doubt he wants a roommate who's going to spy on him in the shower."

"Hey, I would not do that."

Finn raised an eyebrow.

"I mean, I don't *think* I would do that."

Finn shut his laptop. "You made up with Mom, and now you've got a great job. Seems like everything is falling into place for you."

"Now I just need to get laid." I pulled out my phone and called Pepper. "I got it!" I shouted into the phone before she even had the chance to say anything.

"Really?" she said in excitement. "Oh, that's so great. I'm happy for you."

"Let's go out tonight. Hit the bars. I want a drink in my hand and a guy in my bed tonight."

She chuckled. "Ambitious, huh?"

"Very. I'll tell Zach, and you tell the girls."

"I'm on it."

I hung up and turned to Finn. "Want to go out with us tonight?"

He eyed his paperwork. "I've got a lot of stuff to do."

"Come on, celebrate with me. Your brother is getting his life together. We need to commemorate the occasion."

"You don't need to invite me just because we're living together. I understand you have your own friends and your own life."

I raised an eyebrow, having no idea what that meant. "Huh? I consider you to be a friend too. I'm glad that we're closer now. I would have invited you even if I lived somewhere else."

Finn tilted his head slightly. "Really?"

I'd never heard Finn express an ounce of doubt about who he was. He didn't care what people thought of him, especially me. "You're, like, the coolest person I know. Of course I want to hang out with you. And since I don't have to compete with you for girls, that makes it a little easier."

He finally chuckled. "Alright, you convinced me. But I'm not the coolest person you know."

"Then who is?" Zach was awesome, but there wasn't anything special about him.

He rose to his feet and stacked his papers together. "Pepper."

WE MET everyone at the bar. I was dressed in a collared shirt and dark jeans, but Finn didn't own anything nicer than a t-shirt so that's what he wore. He didn't need anything nicer because his rugged good looks and masculine tattoos did all the work for him.

We walked inside and found them sitting at our favorite booth in the corner. Zach was there, sitting close to Stella like he was still working on sealing the deal with her. They were always back and forth. She played games, and Zach always fell for her ploys. Tatum wore a gold dress with nude pumps, her hair pulled back slightly. But Pepper looked like a pinup model in her little black dress and wavy dark hair. Skintight, the dress showed all of her curves and left nothing to the imagination. In silver heels with a matching clutch, she was hogging the attention of every single guy in the building.

When Pepper saw me, she got out of the booth first and opened her arms to me. "Congratulations!"

"Thanks." I moved into her embrace and hugged her tightly. "They offered me the job on the spot. I couldn't believe it."

"I can." She pulled away and kissed me on the cheek. "When do you start?"

"Well, I have to do training all next week. And then I start next Monday."

"Where's your training?"

"Southern California. At first, I was excited to travel there, but then I realized I'm going by myself, so it won't be that great."

The excitement melted off her face. "So you're going to be out of town for an entire week?"

"Yeah. Why?"

"I just... That's a long time."

I shrugged. "At least I'm getting paid for it, right?"

"Yeah..."

I moved to Zach next and hugged him. "You're buying my drinks tonight, right?"

"Yeah, I guess so," he said. "You deserve it."

I hugged the girls then turned back to Pepper.

She was staring at Finn, neither happy nor sad to see him. It was just a stare, the same kind he gave to people, a look that was moody and unreadable.

He gave her the same stare in return—like he loved and hated her at the same time.

5

PEPPER

I felt Finn stare at me, his eyes roaming over my curves in my dress like he didn't give a damn if anyone saw. When his eyes met mine, that same ferocity was in his gaze, like he was pissed at me, when I'd done nothing to deserve his anger. It always seemed to be that way with us, like we were in a twisted game.

He stepped toward me, and his fingers brushed against my wrist. "Can I get you a drink?"

It was a harmless question, but with that deep voice and the slight shadow on his jaw, it seemed far from innocent. "Martini."

He moved to Stella and Tatum. "Girls, you want anything?"

Stella was still mad about his rejection, so she brushed him off. "There's plenty of other men in here who would be happy to get me a drink."

"Like me." Zach leaned in. "I'll get you whatever you want, baby."

"Lemon drop," she answered.

Zach took off like a dog fetching a ball.

Finn turned to Tatum as if nothing had happened. "What about you?"

"I'll have a martini too," she answered.

"Coming right up." Finn turned away.

"Whoa, what about me?" Colton asked. "I'm the man of the hour, right?"

"You're already living with me rent-free," Finn said as he glanced at his brother. "I'll tell Zach to get you something." He walked to the bar, looking like a walking orgasm. Every woman in the bar was aware of him the second he walked inside. I was hoping he wouldn't come out tonight because I didn't want to watch him leave with someone else.

But now that Colton was going to be gone for an entire week, completely out of the state, I feared that even more. Finn would be home alone with no witnesses keeping tabs on him. And I would be alone too.

We'd been struggling to restrain ourselves lately. Like two horny teenagers waiting for their parents to go out of town, once the opportunity presented itself, we would be too emotional to think straight.

I couldn't let that happen.

Zach returned from the bar far quicker than Finn

did. "Colton, if you really want to get laid tonight, maybe we should go to a gay bar."

"I love gay bars!" Stella threw her hand in the air. "So much more fun than regular bars."

I didn't hate the idea—especially since there would be fewer women to hit on Finn. When I looked at the bar, I already spotted a woman sinking her claws into him, her hand resting on his forearm as he waited for the bartender to finish making our drinks.

The man couldn't go anywhere without pussy being thrown at him.

God, it was annoying.

It was even more annoying that I cared. "I'm always down for whatever."

"What do you think, Colton?" Tatum asked.

He shrugged. "I've never been to a gay bar. That could be fun."

"I say we do it." He turned to Stella. "But I don't want the dudes to think I'm available, so I'm gonna need to rub up on you a little bit."

"That's fine with me," she said with a shrug.

Zach stared at her in surprise before he turned to Colton. "I love having Finn around. Stella gets mad and is all over me trying to prove something to him. It's perfect."

Stella didn't correct him.

"What about Finn?" Tatum asked. "Once he walks into that bar, he's gonna be swarmed by dicks."

"No, he's not," Colton said quickly. "Any guy who lays eyes on him knows he's straight. He's as straight as a line."

"Hey, what about me?" Zach asked in offense.

"You know what I mean," Colton said. "Finn is..."

"Masculine, rugged, quiet, cold," I blurted, knowing exactly what he was talking about.

Colton snapped his fingers. "Exactly. If anything, all the women there will be all over him."

I couldn't stop myself from sighing in frustration. When I turned back around, Finn finally left the bar, leaving the woman behind.

Thank god.

He handed Tatum and me our drinks before he sipped his scotch.

"Are you cool with going to a gay bar?" Tatum asked. "Colton wants to get laid."

Finn held his glass at his stomach, perfectly straight with rigid shoulders. The metal chain from his military dog tags was visible around his neck before it disappeared under his shirt. "I don't care where we go."

"Even if dudes hit on you?" Zach asked.

Finn held his gaze, not having a reaction in the slightest. "Wouldn't be the first time."

JUST AS I FEARED, the women swarmed him there too.

It pissed me off, but I couldn't blame them. If I saw him in a bar, I would do the exact same thing.

Colton was talking to a guy at the bar, and Zach and Stella were making out in a booth. Stella kept opening her eyes and glancing in Finn's direction, hoping to spot him staring.

Finn didn't care about a lot of things, but he definitely didn't care about her.

I didn't have the heart to tell her that.

Tatum flirted with the bartender, so I drank alone, watching everyone dance in the middle of the club and have a good time. I forced myself not to look at Finn because I didn't want to torture myself. Seeing women grope him in public as they tried to take him home got under my skin. It was unfair. If my ex weren't his brother, I could be taking him right now. Not only did my husband leave me for other men, but he was the very reason I couldn't have what I wanted most.

It seemed like the universe purposely conspired against me.

"If this were a straight bar, you would not be alone right now." Finn appeared at my side, holding a glass of scotch in his hand. He set it on the table and stood beside me.

"This isn't a straight bar, and you aren't alone right now."

"I'm not alone because I'm with you." He pivoted

his body slightly toward me, his blue eyes glowing in the dim lighting.

Every woman probably hated me right now. "Get a lot of phone numbers?"

"I don't usually ask for phone numbers. Numbers mean there's texting. And when there's texting, there's no fucking. I prefer to take them home then and there, and be done with it."

He was such a pig, but at least he was honest about it. "Who are you taking home tonight?"

He stared me down with his fingers wrapped around his glass. "You."

I felt my pulse quicken in my neck, felt the blood pound in my ears. Even over the loud music, I could feel it. "Is that so?"

"Yes. I'm not letting you take an Uber home dressed like that."

"What makes you think I won't go home with anybody?"

His eyes narrowed, like the suggestion pissed him off. "Because no other man will go near you while I stand here. And I'll stand here all night."

I had to break the connection because the contact was too much. This man said the sexiest things, things my former lovers never said to me. He was the only man who could pull off lines like that.

He leaned in closer to me, maybe because the music was too loud, or maybe it was just an excuse.

"You look beautiful. When I first saw you tonight, both of my hands tightened into fists because all I could think was about was yanking that dress off you."

I'd been jealous of the women making passes at him, but they were the ones who should have been jealous of me, apparently. "Don't torture me..."

He glanced down at my body. "You're the one torturing me." His arm moved around my waist and rested against the small of my back, fitting there perfectly like my curves were made for him to touch.

"Let's not forget what we decided on."

He kept his face close to mine as he listened. "Do you want me to go home with someone else tonight?"

I could barely tolerate it when women bought him a drink.

"Answer me, baby."

"You already know what my answer is."

"I want to hear you say it anyway." He brought me into him closer, his large hand spanning across my narrow back.

"I'm your brother's ex-wife—"

"Say it."

"No," I hissed through my teeth. "No, I don't..."

His lips were practically on mine. "I don't want you to be with that guy across the hall."

"I figured..."

Neither one of us seemed to care if anyone noticed our closeness. We continued to stand huddled together, close enough for a kiss. His hand stayed on my back, controlling and possessive. He held me exactly the way a woman should be held.

"This is going down a path neither one of us wants to take. We're becoming people we don't want to be. We talked about this..."

"I know," he said. "But no amount of talking can stop this from happening. It's already happened, it's already begun. This is beyond restraint. This is beyond our control. I haven't been with a woman since the day you broke up with Jax. I'm not faithful to you because we're in a relationship. I'm celibate because you're the only woman I want, and anyone else will just be a disappointment."

"It's wrong—"

"It's so fucking wrong. But as time keeps passing, it feels less wrong. It feels right."

"It doesn't change anything. Colton would never be okay with this."

"Then he doesn't need to find out."

I looked into his eyes, the implication washing over me. Were we prepared to tiptoe behind his back, be the kind of monsters that hid in the shadows? "I don't know if I can do that..."

"It's gonna happen anyway. Tonight, we can agree to just be friends, but we both know that won't last. I don't know when or how it'll happen, but it'll happen. This beyond both of us. I'm a man of honor, integrity, and honesty, but when it comes to you...all that shit goes out the window."

I knew I should just walk away, but I was huddled close to him like I had no intention of leaving. Now I was an accomplice in this betrayal.

"He's the one who threw you away. He's the one who ended it."

"Doesn't change the fact that I was his wife. You can spin it however you want, but we both know it's wrong."

"I know how wrong it is. Doesn't change the way I feel."

My eyes shifted back and forth as I looked into his.

"I tried. I really did. But once Jax was gone...I lost all self-control."

"I don't want to be a liar. I don't want to sneak around behind his back—"

"Neither do I."

"Then maybe we should talk to him."

He shook his head. "We both know what his answer is going to be. And he has every right to give that answer. I'd rather have you for a short period of time than not have you at all. To enjoy you while we burn like a white-hot inferno. When the flames go out and it turns dark, we walk away. Maybe that will be enough for us to move on."

"Or maybe it'll make us want each other even more..."

6

COLTON

Tom rubbed my arm before he turned back to the bar. "I'll pay the tab, and we'll get out of here." When he turned away, I could see his muscular back stretched out his t-shirt, and his jeans were snug on that perfect ass.

This was really happening.

I was about to get laid.

"I'll be right back." I stepped away and found Finn and Pepper standing together at a table. They were close together, as if they were having an intimate conversation like a pair of lovers.

"Guys, I need to talk to you." I broke up their conversation and got right between them, the two best-looking people in the bar. Pepper looked like she belonged on a magazine cover in that black dress, and my brother's masculinity was even more intense in a gay bar.

Pepper stepped away from Finn then grabbed her glass. She took a drink and finished it off before returning it to the table. "What's up?"

Finn continued to hold his scotch at his waist, as perfectly comfortable in a gay bar as he was in a straight one. He was probably talking to Pepper like that so the guys would assume he was off-limits.

"I met this sexy dude named Tom. He asked me if I want to get out of here." Aaron was the last thing on my mind now that I had another fish on my line. He'd never texted me back, and now that I'd put myself out there, I realized there were so many options. I didn't need to wait around for Aaron. "He's paying the tab right now, then we're going to leave."

"So why are you talking to us?" Finn asked. "We should be the last thing on your mind."

"I don't know... I guess I'm just nervous." I couldn't stand still, so I constantly shifted my weight then looked over my shoulder to make sure Tom wasn't waiting for me. "I've never done this before. This guy is handsome and funny...he's the whole package."

"Just be confident," Pepper said. "That's what attracted me to you when we first met. You were so suave and easygoing. Just don't take it too seriously. Have fun with it. Enjoy it."

I turned to my brother. "Any advice?"

"I've never fucked a dude, so no. But what Pepper said is pretty good."

"God, I'm so nervous right now." I shook out my hands.

"Take Pepper's advice," my brother said. "Sex is better when both partners are confident and passionate. No one wants to sleep with a timid and self-conscious lover. The only way you could be a better lover is by not retreating or acting uncertain. So don't shake your hands out and seem afraid. Act like there's nothing else you want more than this guy."

"Well...there is nothing I want more at the moment." I'd watched enough gay porn to last a lifetime. I was ready for the real thing, to feel a man's hands on my body. I wanted to feel the muscles of his shoulders and kiss those soft lips like there was no tomorrow.

"Then show it," Finn said seriously. "Have fun."

"How do you pick up so many women all the time?" I asked. "Women you don't even know. Aren't you nervous?"

Finn seemed like the question made him uncomfortable, which was unusual for him. "It's just sex. I don't overthink it. You shouldn't either."

"Alright. Wish me luck." I started to walk away, but I turned back around when I remembered something. "Finn, can you make sure Pepper gets home okay? I don't want her taking a taxi looking like a supermodel."

She raised an eyebrow as she looked at me. "I can get home on my own—"

"I'll take care of it." Finn patted me on the shoulder. "Have fun."

"Thanks." I gave them a thumbs-up before I walked away. I stopped by Zach's table and saw him locked in a heated embrace with Stella. "I'm going home with a stud tonight."

Zach didn't stop kissing Stella. All he could manage was a thumbs-up as he kept his eyes closed and sucked her face.

"You two have fun." I knew that relationship was based on a twisted premise, but Zach wanted her so bad, he didn't care if he was being used. If anything, he *wanted* to be used. I headed back to the bar and found Tom.

"There you are," he said, smiling wide. "I was worried you got started without me."

I'd gotten started by myself long enough. "Never."

7

PEPPER

I sat in the middle seat because Tatum was against the window. As a result, my thigh touched Finn's, and I could feel his muscular arm against my own. He didn't wear cologne because his natural scent was more than enough. I loved that smell. Every time it entered my nose, I imagined him naked in the shower.

Even though I imagined him naked all the time anyway.

"It didn't work out with the bartender?" I asked.

"He doesn't get off until two, so I told him to swing by when his shift is over." Her blond hair was in a slick ponytail, so her slender neck was on display. Hoop earrings dangled from her lobes, adding to her classy appearance.

"That should be fun."

"You didn't see anyone you liked?" she asked. "Or are you still into Jax?"

I hadn't thought about Jax much lately. The only man on my mind was the one sitting beside me. He was in my thoughts at work, at home, and in my sleep. "No. Jax and I were never going to work out. That relationship was doomed to fail from the beginning."

"Too bad," she said as she looked out the window. "He was hot."

Not as hot as Finn.

"But you'll find someone else," Tatum said. "You can have whoever you want, Pepper. And when you're finally ready, you can go and pick him out."

It was ironic, because I couldn't have the one man I actually wanted. When I thought about Finn, I never felt like I wasn't ready to be with someone. I was ready to give myself completely to him, mind, body, and soul. When I thought about all the other men on the planet, I didn't feel ready at all. "Yeah...maybe."

Finn pulled up to her apartment building. He didn't get out and walk her to her door the way he did with me. All he said was goodnight before he pulled onto the road.

I prepared to slide over to the seat by the window.

With one hand on the wheel, he grabbed my arm and pulled me back to his side. He kept his eyes on the road and didn't admonish me verbally.

I didn't defy his wishes.

His hand returned to his thigh, and he didn't try to touch me. He just liked having me there, his thigh touching mine. He kept his eyes on the road and didn't fill the silence with conversation. It made it more tense that way, but also more comfortable.

I kept my hands in my lap and resisted the urge to touch him. Colton had gone home with someone, so I felt like I had every right to do the same. Our marriage was over, and now we were just friends. Would it be that terrible if I wanted to be with Finn? I knew the hormones were clouding my judgment because that wasn't rational thinking. Colton had always felt over-shadowed by his older brother, that his parents preferred Finn to him, and if I wanted to be with Finn, it would be a betrayal. Zach was also off-limits, but I'd never been tempted with that option.

"Jax was never man enough for you." His masculine voice broke through the silence. As always, the radio wasn't on, and we sat in silence. Only the sound of traffic and the engine accompanied our moment.

I liked the jealousy in his voice because it made me feel less alone. Every time I saw a woman buy him a drink and tug down her dress another inch to show more cleavage, I died a little inside. This man wasn't mine, but I felt like I owned a piece of him.

"A real man isn't threatened by anyone, especially a gay ex-husband. A real man isn't worried his woman will cheat because he knows she'll find no one better.

A real man doesn't ask his woman to make sacrifices. He's the one who makes the sacrifices."

Jesus, this man was sexy. He said the most romantic things even though he'd never been with a woman for longer than a weekend. "I knew you never liked him..."

"Why would I like a man who's not good enough for you?"

"Is there any man good enough for me?"

He kept his eyes on the road, one hand on the wheel. His eyes hardly blinked as he considered the question. "Me."

I wanted to smother myself into his side and kiss his neck. I wanted to wrap my arms around his hard body and never let go. I wanted him to pull over to a random curb so he could yank up my dress and thrust inside me.

I'd never felt like this in my entire life. I'd never had this passion with Colton or Jax. With Finn, I felt a relentless need to have him. Even if it was wrong on so many levels, it didn't seem to matter. It only made me want him more.

He parked at the curb outside my apartment and killed the engine.

"I don't want you to walk me to my door." Every time we stood in that hallway, something bad happened. His hand dug into my hair, and he held me like a man held a woman. A sensual hug might turn into a kiss. And a kiss could turn into something much worse.

He eyed me as he slipped his keys into his pocket. "I don't care what you want, baby." He opened the door and got out.

I wanted to remain behind in defiance, but it was cold and I wore almost nothing. I got out of the truck and felt his arm slide around my waist as he brought me close.

I didn't push him away. It was nice to feel his touch, his protective embrace. I moved closer into him, knowing how it felt to be the other women he took home on the weekends. I just wished this night would end with him between my legs, every fat inch making me howl like a banshee.

He guided me up the stairs and to my front door. I wanted to get the door unlocked so I could dart inside, but he would probably follow me. And if we were alone in an apartment together, nothing good would happen. I turned around and kept my back to the door. "Thanks for driving me home."

His eyes watched my lips move as he leaned in closer to me.

I moved back, but my ass bumped into the door.

He came closer, his chest pressing against mine as his arms slid around my waist. He tightened his grip and pulled me more firmly against him, making my back arch deeper. His nose rubbed against mine, and it seemed like he might kiss me.

"No." It was the only coherent word I could blurt out of my mouth.

His mouth moved to my neck, and he kissed me passionately, his full lips dragging against my skin and his tongue tasting me. His hand dug into the back of my hair, and he kept me still as he devoured me.

I closed my eyes and enjoyed it, wishing we were both naked.

He pressed me against the door and kept kissing me, like there were no more lines to cross.

It would be easy for me to get the door unlocked and invite him inside, but I found the courage to resist him. I pressed my hand against his chest and pushed him back. "No. This isn't going to happen, Finn."

"It's already happening, baby." He pulled away and looked me in the eye, the hunger burning in his gaze. "But we'll do it your way." He stepped back so there was some space between us. "You know where to find me when you change your mind."

8

COLTON

"What about this one?" I stepped out of the changing room in the collared shirt. It was gray and fitted, and it looked good with jeans and slacks.

"I like it." Pepper looked me up and down with her arms crossed over her chest. "It'll be perfect."

"Awesome." I walked back inside, changed back into my clothes, and then carried my stuff to the register. I would be doing training all week in San Diego, and I needed some new clothes. I'd lost some weight since leaving my old firm, and I wanted to make a good impression. The clerk charged everything, and I put it on a credit card. "Thanks for shopping with me today."

"No problem," she said. "I want you to look your best."

I grabbed all the bags and walked out with her.

"Too bad that apartment is already taken. I wish I could move back there."

"Well...you never know. I suppose I could be really weird and drive him out of the apartment."

"I'd rather you sleep with him, have a relationship, and then dump him so it's really awkward and he has to move."

"That seems mean..."

"He'd get laid, wouldn't he?"

"You could just move back in with me," she suggested.

It wasn't the worst idea, but I knew that wouldn't be appropriate. "I'm sure I'll find something. I just really liked that apartment."

"Yeah, I know what you mean."

We got into the back of the taxi and then headed to Finn's house.

"So, you never told me what happened with Tom," she said, giving me a knowing look.

A blush entered my cheeks. "You really want to know?" I was open-minded about her sex life, but I didn't want to hear all the details. This woman used to be my wife, the person I slept with every night. I doubt she wanted to hear me desire a man in a way I never desired her.

"Of course. We're friends now. It really doesn't bother me."

I was glad we were finally in that place. "Well...it

was pretty awesome." A smile stretched my mouth apart as I couldn't keep a straight face. "I took your advice and stayed confident. He didn't know that it was my first time, and I don't think I gave him any clues. We're going out again when I get back to town."

"That's awesome," she said, sounding sincere. "Is it everything you wanted it to be?"

I didn't know how it would go. The only experience I had was through porn. "I'm definitely gay... I'll leave it at that."

She chuckled. "I can tell by that stupid smile on your face. I've never seen you happier."

The comment made me sad because it was true. I was happy on my wedding day. I was happy every day in my marriage. But there had always been something missing. Now I finally found it.

We arrived at Finn's house and walked inside.

In just his sweatpants, he was doing one-arm push-ups on the rug in front of the fireplace. With one hand behind his back, he slowly lowered himself to the floor then pushed back up. His body was coated with sweat, and his arms were swollen with the exerted muscle.

Pepper stopped and stared at him, her jaw practically on the floor.

I wasn't surprised because I was used to seeing this every day. "He likes to show off."

Finn turned his head and glanced at us as he finished one more push-up. He pushed off the ground and rose to his feet. His eyes went to Pepper first, his blue eyes vibrant from the exercise he'd just completed. With abs so chiseled they looked like small rocks, he walked toward us, still looking at Pepper. "Shopping?"

"I got some clothes for my trip," I answered, even though Finn treated me like I wasn't in the room. "Pepper helped me pick out a few things. I may be a gay man, but I don't have great taste in clothes."

With his hands on his hips, he finally turned to me. "When do you leave?"

"Tomorrow morning."

"You need a lift to the airport?"

"You aren't working?" I asked.

"Later in the day."

"Then that would be cool," I said. "Thanks."

Finn turned his attention back to Pepper.

"Are you nervous?" Pepper asked, ignoring his stare and looking at me.

"A bit," I said. "I'm nervous because I really want this to work out. We'll basically be suing companies and corporations that violate the environmental laws of the country, so I won't be dealing with small cases anymore. I'll always be part of a legal team, which will be nice. And I actually care about what I'm fighting for. I never cared about real estate, the rich moguls and their mansions." I rolled my eyes. "Rich bitch problems don't interest me."

Finn reluctantly pulled his gaze away from Pepper's face. "And what about Tom? Does he know you'll be gone?"

"Yeah, I said I would see him when I get back. If this goes somewhere, I'd like you to meet him." He and Pepper would get along great. It wasn't as obvious with Finn since my brother wasn't a big talker.

"And we would love to get to know him," Pepper said.

Finn walked into the kitchen, his body still glistening with sweat. "I was about to make dinner. You guys wanna join?"

"You know I'm always down for free food," I said. "And if Pepper doesn't eat here, she'll starve tonight, unless she stops by Mega Shake on the way home."

She gave me an angry glare. "I'll take your new clothes with me and throw them in the trash on the way."

Finn grabbed the ingredients from the fridge and laid everything out on the counter. "I'll cook for three. Maybe you guys will be done arguing by the time it's ready."

"You don't know us very well," I said with a chuckle. "We never stop arguing."

FINN DROVE me to the airport early in the morning.

"Thanks for the ride," I said. "I know it's early."

"It's fine." He sipped his black coffee out of his thermos. "I'm awake this early anyway. I'll hit the gym after I drop you off, then head to work."

"Does it suck working twelve-hour shifts all the time?" I asked. "That's such a long day."

He shrugged. "I used to work for days at a time in the military—with no sleep. Plus, when I work twelve-hour shifts, I only have to work three days a week. That's a fair trade to me."

"But you usually work more than three days a week." It seemed like four or five.

"That's only because we're backed up with patients. Not enough ER docs in the area to serve the population."

"Hmm...maybe I should have been a doctor."

He scoffed, like the suggestion was absurd.

"What?" I asked, mildly offended. "You don't think I'm smart enough? I graduated from law school."

"You nearly vomit anytime you get a little cut."

"But that's different. That's my blood. It's weird."

He shook his head. "I had a patient come in with multiple stab wounds the other night. I had to give him a transfusion because he'd lost so much blood. If you can't handle a cut on your hand, you wouldn't have been able to handle that."

Alright, he had a point. "I'll stick with being a lawyer, then..."

"Good call." He pulled into the terminal and stopped in front of the airline I was taking. "You'll be gone for a whole week? I'm excited to have the house to myself for once."

"Yes, I'm sure you'll have a fuck-a-thon."

He dropped his playful attitude as he watched me grab my suitcase from behind the seat.

I came back to the window and waved. "Thanks for the ride, man. I'll see you when I get back."

He raised his hand. "Yeah...I'll see you then."

It seemed like he wanted to say something more, but since this was an unloading zone only, I knew we couldn't have a long conversation. I waved and walked off.

I CHECKED in to my hotel and hung up my new clothes in the closet.

Zach called me, so I took the call as I organized my things. "Hey, what's up?"

"Are you in San Diego already?"

"Yep. Just unpacking my stuff. What's up?"

"Not sure what to do about Stella."

"Last time I saw you guys, you were going at it like dogs in the back of the club."

"Yeah, and it was super-hot. But she seems to only care about that dumb asshole brother of yours."

I talked shit about my brother from time to time, but it was always in a playful way. I didn't tolerate any insults directed at my family, even if it was a joke or pent-up anger. "Don't call my brother an asshole, alright?" He wasn't just a veteran, but a loyal brother. And even if he weren't those things, I would still defend him.

"I'm just frustrated that Stella is still hung up on him. I mean, I'm glad she's using me to make him jealous, but when he's not around, she drops me. It's annoying."

"You knew from the beginning Stella didn't want you. She's just using you."

"Yeah, but I want her to keep using me."

"But since that's not going to go anywhere, do you still want to do that?"

He was quiet for a long time. "This is Stella we're talking about. She's fucking gorgeous. Of course I want her in any way I can get her."

"Well, she's egotistical. So if you really want a shot at her, you should drop her."

"What?" he asked in surprise. "You kidding me?"

"Just like with Finn, drop her and seem indifferent. She'll be wounded by your rejection, so she'll actually want you to want her. Then she'll chase you."

"Or make out with some other guy to make me jealous..."

"I doubt it. She'll make a move first."

"That's not a bad idea, Colton. Thanks for the advice."

"No problem." I looked through my suitcase and searched for my notes. The company asked me to prepare a few things for the meeting, but they were nowhere to be found. I removed all my clothes and hair products and realized they weren't there.

Then I remembered where I left them.

On my bed.

"Shit, I've got to go, Zach." Without waiting for him to respond, I hung up and called Finn.

It went to voice mail.

I forgot he was at work. I called Pepper next.

"Hey, I need a favor," I blurted. "I was an idiot and left all my paperwork behind on my bed."

"So you brought all your new clothes but forgot the one thing you actually needed?" she asked sarcastically.

"I don't have time for this. I need you to go to Finn's place, grab the papers, and one-day ship them to me."

"Why don't you just have Finn do it?"

"He's at work."

"Ooh...well, I don't have a key."

"There's a spare in the flowerpot by the door. You'll do this for me, right?"

She sighed like it was the last thing she wanted to do, which was strange because she never minded helping me with anything. "Yeah, sure. But you're sure Finn isn't home? I don't want to just barge in on him."

"Yes. When he dropped me off, he said he had to work, and he's not answering his phone."

"Alright."

"And he wouldn't care if you showed up anyway. This is important."

She didn't respond to that. "I'll swing by when I get off work."

"But that's in two hours..."

"It's not going to get there any faster if I pick it up in two hours."

"Yeah, I guess that's true..."

"Honestly, it's three o' clock now, so it wouldn't get processed until tomorrow anyway. So would that even work?"

"The meeting isn't until Tuesday, so if you could ship it out first thing in the morning, that could work."

"Alright. I'll do it Tuesday morning, then."

"Thanks so much, Pepper. I owe you one."

"Oh, Colton...you owe me more than just one."

9

PEPPER

The Uber dropped me off at the house, and I walked to the front door. The only reason I agreed to this was because Finn wasn't there. There was no way I would walk into the house if it would be just the two of us. With couches, beds, and booze everywhere, it couldn't end well. My panties would be flung onto the lamp, and the rest of my clothes would be spread out everywhere else, like eggs hidden on Easter Sunday.

I found the key in the flowerpot then let myself inside. It was dead quiet, so it seemed like I was alone. I took the stairs to the second floor and made my way down the hallway. I'd been to the second floor once before when I was picking out his furniture, but I hadn't been there since. The master bedroom belonged to Finn, so one of these spare rooms must be Colton's.

A door opened, and footsteps sounded a second later.

Shit.

When the footsteps stopped, I knew he was standing right behind me. I didn't want to turn around and face him, see those pretty blue eyes look at me with such imminent desire. That man could reduce me to skin, bone, and hormones with just a look.

I slowly turned around. When I laid my eyes on him, I knew I was in serious trouble.

He stood with a towel around his waist, his skin covered in droplets from the shower. His hair was slightly damp and messy, like he'd rubbed the towel on his scalp before securing it around his narrow hips. Tanned skin was prevalent under the dark ink. His hard chest led to narrow hips, and farther down, to a perfectly manicured happy trail, a chiseled V in his hips, and a prominent vein emerging from underneath the towel.

Double shit.

With his chiseled arms hanging by his sides, he stared me down with that same look he gave me in public and behind closed doors. He didn't seem to care that I'd broken in to his house and trespassed on his property without permission. It was an afterthought to him.

Seeing him practically naked put me in a fog. I'd seen him shirtless more often than dressed, but seeing him in that short little towel that showed off his muscular thighs and calves was like dangling crack in front of an addict. "What are you doing here?" I blurted out the question, so unnerved that I couldn't think of something better to say

His right eyebrow rose slowly. "I live here."

"Colton said you were at work." I crossed my arms over my chest, like that would protect me from this threat.

He slowly walked toward me, his footsteps muffled by the new carpet.

Oh no.

His eyes were focused on my face as if an invisible target was on my forehead. He moved slowly, a predator carefully approaching its prey. "It was slow at the hospital. I came home early."

"But it's never slow..." He told me he had to work late all the time because there weren't enough doctors to serve the population. On average, he was stuck in the ER for an extra three hours for every shift, and he got called in all the time. And it just had to be slow today? The universe was seriously conspiring against me. I was alone in the house with him, Colton was two states away, and Finn was dressed in a little towel with drops of water on his shoulders.

He stopped in front of me, his hand moving to my neck.

I couldn't let this happen. His fingertips felt searing hot against my skin, and the scent of his soap lowered my inhibitions better than booze. If I didn't get out of there now, I'd end up naked on his bed—and I would never leave. I stepped back. "Finn, no—"

He grabbed his towel and yanked it off his waist.

My eyes immediately went down south.

He dropped the towel onto the ground and stood there proudly, his eyes watching my reaction.

I couldn't resist a look at the monster between his legs. Long, thick, and perfectly groomed, he had a package he should be proud of. It was a woman's dream, a cock that was just impressively thick as it was long. It was semi-hard, getting harder the longer I stared at his formidable size. "Uh...wow." I swallowed the lump in my throat then lifted my gaze to meet his.

He wore the same dark expression, like he wasn't going to let me leave that house until he'd finally had me. He closed the distance between us then dug his hand deep into my hair. He yanked on the strands and tilted my chin up so he could stare down at me, like an animal that was about to attack another. He claimed me with his look, telling me that I was his. Even if he let go, I wouldn't walk away. He angled his neck down and kissed me, pressing those beautiful full lips against mine.

And took my breath away.

The second he'd dropped that towel, my restraint disappeared. Now that we were locked in a heated embrace, I definitely couldn't walk away. My mind and body both accepted defeat. I slid my hands up his slightly wet chest as I returned his kiss, feeling the same passion as I did the last time we were locked together.

His hands yanked up my shirt so they could slide across the bare skin of my back. His fingers dug into me as he squeezed me, pulled me against his chest, and the hard dick between us kept us slightly apart.

He held me as if I was his, as if there was never a woman before me.

Never a woman after me.

His kiss was slow and patient, a gentle landing that defied the intensity in his gaze. It was a wet, open-mouthed kiss, a sexy exchange of lips and tongue. Every time he breathed into my mouth, a gentle shiver ran down my spine all the way to my ass. His hand moved to the back of my neck, and he supported my head as he kissed me deeper, tugged on my bottom lip with his teeth before his tongue was back in my mouth.

Now I was lost.

Nothing could pull me away from this man. There was no amount of loyalty that could make me do the right thing. This was the one thing my heart desired most, the man who had conquered my body with a single kiss. He infected my soul so deeply that I was never clean no matter how many times I showered. The connection was strong, stronger than anything else I'd ever felt with another man...even my husband.

He barely broke our kiss as he pulled my shirt over my head. The cotton caught my hair and tugged it up before it fell back down again. My shirt dropped to the ground, and his kiss overpowered my lips. He kissed me like it was his last day on this earth. He kissed me like he'd never wanted another woman more. His hand glided into my hair and kept it out of my face as his lips danced with mine, so erotic and seductive. He sucked my bottom lip again as his fingers worked my bra and unclasped it with no effort.

It fell to the ground along with my shirt.

He pulled me harder into his chest so my tits pressed against his warm pecs. I could feel how blazingly hot he was, how sexy it felt to be near him this way. Our hearts were close together, and there was nothing keeping us apart. Skin-on-skin, we were a man and a woman wrapped up so deeply in each other.

He didn't break our kiss to look at me, more enthused by my lips than anything else.

I was so wet that I felt my panties weighed down in my jeans. I could feel the slickness start to drip to my thighs when I imagined this beautiful man inside me. Just our kiss was incredible. Imagine how it would be when we were two naked bodies thrusting on a bed of soft sheets.

He breathed into my mouth before he pulled away and lowered himself to the ground. His powerful arms scooped under my ass and lifted me into the air. Our chests were connected once more, and he kissed me as he carried me to his large bed. The curtains were closed, and it was dark in his bedroom. My back hit the sheets of his king-size bed as he unfastened my jeans and tore them off my legs.

When he grabbed my panties, I lifted my hips and helped him get them off, unwilling to stop for anything at this point. Colton could walk into the house, and I would still give in to this man and deal with the consequences later.

When he pulled down my panties, he saw the sticky slickness as it stretched apart. A focused look came over his face, a sexy expression as he pressed his lips tightly together in noticeable arousal.

He moved on top of me and finally looked at me, his eyes trailing over my perky tits and flat stomach. His mouth moved to the valley between my tits, and he kissed the area softly, smelling my perfume at the same time. His hand groped my right tit, and his thumb flicked over the nipple.

I took a deep breath as I felt him worship my body with his mouth. I was eager to skip to the finale, to feel that large dick inside me. But he purposely made me wait, purposely stretched it out even though I was so damn wet.

His kisses moved to my stomach, and his tongue dived into my belly button as his hand continued to grope my tits.

My hands dug into his hair as my legs wrapped around his hips, a complete mess of hormones on his sheets. There had to be hundreds of women who'd come before me, who'd sweated right against these sheets, but that moment in time felt special, like I meant more than they ever did. "Stop torturing me..." My fingers felt his powerful shoulders, felt the hard muscle underneath that soft skin. My touch grazed over the tattoo of an army tank. It had numbers in the corner, and I wondered if that was the exact tank he'd been in during his service.

He pulled his mouth from my stomach and held himself directly over me, that fierce look in his eyes. "You've been torturing me every day, baby." His thighs separated mine, and he brought our bodies into position.

Finally. My hands dragged down his back as I brought him close to me, my pussy clenching in preparation for what was about to happen. The weight of his muscles pressed me into the mattress, made the sheets cup my body as he suffocated me with his presence. His muscular thighs brushed against mine as he prepared to take me, prepared to cross the line in a way he could never take back.

I didn't have any hesitation at all. It didn't matter how wrong it was. It didn't matter how much I would regret it the next time I was thinking clearly. I would have this man if it was the last thing I'd do.

He locked his gaze on mine as he pressed his fat head inside, becoming smeared in the slickness that seeped out of my entrance. It coated his head and made the most powerful lubricant in the world. He slowly sank inside me, his big cock stretching me apart because I was wet enough to allow it to happen.

He wasn't even that deep, and it already felt amazing. My hands palmed his chest as I got lost in the lustful goodness. A moment of uncertainly clenched my chest when I realized the crucial step we'd both missed. "Wait...you didn't put on a condom."

He sank deeper into me like he didn't give a damn. "I'm not wearing a condom with you. I'm clean, and you're clean too." He kept sinking farther inside me, his dick inching inside as he kept stretching me.

When he was almost fully sheathed, pragmatism went out the window. I didn't care there was no protection between us. I just wanted this man all the way inside me. My hands gripped his muscular torso, and I pulled him into me, getting the last few inches until he was against my cervix. "Finn..."

He pressed his forehead to mine, and he went still,

his eyes closed and his lips pressed tightly together as he enjoyed the feeling of my bare pussy.

My nails clawed at him because the pleasure was so inexplicably good. Sex had never felt this profound, felt this innately wonderful. My knees were wide apart to give him plenty of room, and I wanted him to fuck me until I couldn't take it anymore. I wanted these sheets to reek of sweat, to smell like good sex.

He pulled away and opened his eyes, a slight tint of redness on his face. His dog tags hung from around his neck and dragged against my chest, sliding right between my tits when he moved. The metal was warm rather than cold, probably because his skin was searing to the touch. "I've wanted to fuck this pussy since the moment I laid eyes on you. Now it's mine." His arms slid behind my knees, and he positioned me to take his dick deep. He slowly thrust inside me, sliding past my wetness as he became more coated with my slickness.

I closed my eyes because it felt so good, so unbelievably good that I didn't know how to react. Sex had been good with Jax, but it had never been like this. Colton had never been like this. No one had been like this.

His lips moved to mine, and he kissed me as he thrust inside me, his powerful body working in the most beautiful way. He moved inside me but kept his body hard and still at the same time.

My hand moved into the back of his hair, feeling the short strands I'd fantasized about. My lips moved with his, and I felt my body betray me so quickly. The burn started in my belly before it reached the area between my legs. Slowly, the fire grew bigger and bigger, approaching a climax that would make my toes curl. I stopped kissing him because my lips stopped working. All I could focus on was the explosion that was about to rip me into a million pieces. My nails dragged down his back, and I pulled him into me harder, my moans beginning as a quiet refrain.

Finn watched me as he thrust harder, knowing I was about to come for him in record time. The man had only been inside me a few seconds, and I was already exploding. Like a horny teenage boy, I couldn't hold back my orgasm.

"Come on, baby." He tilted his hips and rubbed his body against my clit as he moved inside me, giving me the most intoxicating pleasure I'd ever known. His hard body gleamed with a light drizzle of sweat, and he moaned once I hit my threshold.

My nails turned to daggers, and I came around him with a scream. My toes curled as I expected and they started to cramp, but the pain didn't mask the undeniable pleasure. My legs widened farther as I took more of him, coming all over his dick like a hard-up woman. "Finn..." I looked into those blue eyes as I finished, falling so deeply in that moment that my heart increased tenfold. I should be embarrassed by how briefly I lasted, but I didn't feel ashamed with this man. The connection between us was so strong, invisible but prevalent.

When I caught my breath, he kissed me again. His kiss matched the speed of his thrusts, a quick pace that wasn't borderline hasty. Instead of fucking me like I was just a piece of ass, he took me like I was somewhere in between lovemaking and fucking.

It was the best sex I've ever had—hands down.

Naked and coated in sweat, we moved together like there was nowhere else we'd rather be. My panties were on his bedroom floor, and Colton assumed I was here picking up his papers. My phone was in the pocket of my jeans, so if he called, I wouldn't even notice. The second he was gone, I got hot and naked with this beautiful man, enjoying myself so thoroughly I had no idea how I'd ever enjoyed someone else.

I wanted this man to come inside me, to come over and over until he dripped between my thighs. The idea of carrying his seed aroused me in a way it never had with Jax. Jax worked so hard to screw me without a condom, and I resisted as long as I could. But with Finn, there was no resistance at all. I didn't want a piece of latex to separate us. I wanted him, skin-on-skin.

Ten minutes later, he made the impossible possible. He brought me to another orgasm even though nothing had changed. He still rocked into me at the same pace, and he still kissed me with the same vigor. The connection between us was what made me convulse around him so easily. This man could have any other woman in the world—but he wanted me. "Finn..." A man had never made me come more than once. I didn't even think that was possible. But he succeeded with flying colors. "Yes..." I breathed into his mouth as my hands dragged down his back, his tags sliding through the sweat on my chest.

Those blue eyes watched me explode around him a second time, his desire so profound it seemed like he couldn't last much longer. If he hadn't been with anyone for the last six weeks, his restraint was worth a medal.

"Come inside me..." I wanted him to finish, to feel the same pleasure he gave me. He'd certainly earned it, and I wanted to watch him get off. The sight would turn me on, keep me slick and wet for another round once he recovered. My hands gripped his ass and I guided him deeper inside me, wanting him to give it to me good.

He gave me a final kiss before he released. "You want my come, baby?"

"Please..."

He shoved himself completely inside me as he released, balls deep. A masculine moan escaped his throat, and his expression deepened as he filled me, his big cock thickening as the pleasure hit him as hard as it had hit me. His ass tightened and he released another moan, his throat shifting with the noise.

It was so hot.

I wanted this man to come inside me as much as he could.

His body shuddered once he was finished, and his gaze focused once more. He slowly pulled out of me, careful not to take the come with him. Then he rolled over and lay beside me, his sexy body hard and tight from the exertion.

I didn't hesitate before I turned into him and snuggled into his side. My arm hooked around his waist, and I tucked my leg in between his. My face rested against his shoulder, and I closed my eyes, more comfortable than I'd ever been.

He grabbed a pillow from the top of the bed so we could share it. Once he was comfortable, he turned his head my way and placed a kiss on my forehead. No words were said. He didn't ask me why I was in his house. He didn't ask me if I regretted what just happened. We were together, quiet and happy.

I didn't realize how much I wanted this until I finally had it. Finn was more than just a lover and a friend. He was the perfect mixture of both, something my marriage had lacked. He was the person I loved to be around the most, and the sexual attraction I had for him was paramount. Lying against his side was the most comfortable place in the world, the one place I wanted to be.

His hand moved across my cheek then drifted into my hair, pulling it away from my face as he examined me.

I opened my eyes and looked into his blue ones, seeing the same affection and desire in his gaze.

He leaned down and kissed me on the mouth, a kiss so soft that it didn't seem like a man so hard could be so gentle. He pulled away, watched me for a few seconds, and then closed his eyes.

10

PEPPER

My panties were too wet to wear, so I skipped them and pulled on the t-shirt he'd taken out of his drawer. The warm cotton surrounded me, so soft to the touch and pregnant with his laundry detergent. I pulled out my hair that was trapped under the collar and let it hang down my back.

"Looks good on you." Finn came up behind me and drew my hair over one shoulder. His mouth came down on my neck, and he kissed me aggressively, his tongue tasting me in places he'd already explored. His arm hooked around my tits, and he pulled me tightly against him, his warm breath falling across my ear.

My eyes closed, and I let him have me.

When he pulled away, his large hand squeezed my

left ass cheek. Then he gave it a playful smack before he walked away.

This man was doing crazy things to me. I never felt more alive and dead at the same time. I watched his powerful body exit the bedroom, his muscular body disappearing into his gray sweatpants.

I couldn't believe that tattooed piece of man meat was the guy I was sleeping with.

The guy who was making me come.

I left the bedroom and followed him downstairs.

He wordlessly pulled out ingredients from the fridge and got to work preparing dinner. By the looks of it, we were having salmon, rice, and broccoli. He marinated the fish in lemon and spices then placed it in the oven before he put the rice in the rice maker.

"Need help?" I leaned on the counter, his shirt stretching all the way to my knees.

"I like how you offer after I'm done." He met my look with a playful gaze.

"You should be grateful I offered at all."

He washed his hands then came around the counter toward me. With a predatory look in his eyes, he stared at me like I was a wild animal about to get caught in a trap. His arm circled my waist, and he brought me close. "The salmon will take twenty minutes. What should do we in the meantime?"

I had a few ideas. I lifted myself onto the counter and opened my legs.

He didn't hesitate to look at my cunt, to see the white globs of come that stuck to the insides of my thighs. "Good idea." He pushed the front of his sweat-pants down and let his impressive dick pop out. His hands cradled my ass and pulled it to the edge. The counter was in line with his waist, so he didn't struggle to shove himself inside me, giving me a hard thrust that wasn't nearly as gentle as it was when we were in his bedroom.

I gripped his shoulders and held on as he fucked me hard on the counter, pounding his big dick deep inside me like he hadn't just gotten laid several times. I moaned in his face as he took me roughly, stretching my pussy so wide apart it still hadn't gotten used to his size. I could see our reflection in the TV on the wall, seeing his muscular ass flex over and over again as he pounded deep inside me.

I kept my knees wide apart and used his back as an anchor to keep me close. I let him fuck me good and hard, making me come like he hadn't done it earlier at all. I bit my bottom lip and watched his muscular physique work to fuck me on his kitchen counter, just above the drawer with the silverware. "God...yes." My head tilted back as I finished, my cream and his come building up around his length.

He gripped the back of my neck and brought me close. "I love making you come."

"Because it's so easy?"

"Because you look so damn sexy." He didn't break his pace as he spoke, sliding his big cock into my eager cunt without missing a beat.

I didn't look as sexy as he did.

We kept fucking hard on the kitchen counter, ignoring the sound of the rain outside. The water pelted the windows, but we made the temperature of the room rise several degrees. We were covered in sweat all over again even though we had just cooled off.

When the timer went off, Finn slowed down and pushed himself deep inside. Like he was trained to come on command, he filled my pussy with his load as he gave me a heated expression, the same expression he gave when he claimed me in public, the same expression he gave when he saw Damon across the hall. Now he gave it to me again, telling me I was his as his cock pumped me full of his seed.

Not that I wanted to be anyone else's.

He finished with a groan then slowly pulled himself out, his come dripping everywhere because I was so full of his loads. He grabbed a paper towel and wiped my entrance, his gaze hard and his lips pressed hard together in arousal.

Like nothing had happened, he tossed the paper in the garbage and finished preparing dinner. He made two plates before he sat down at the dining table.

Since I didn't have any underwear, I put a few paper towels on the chair before I sat down.

"You can wear some of my boxers if you want."

"Why did you wait so long to offer?"

He took a bite of his fish, taking his time before actually answering. "I like watching my come drip out of your cunt."

Only a hard man like him could pull that off.

I was tired and satisfied, so I ate my dinner slowly and tried not to think about the situation I was in. Now I was officially sleeping with Finn, and I had no idea what would happen next. I wasn't foolish enough to think it would end anytime soon. It seemed to be only beginning. "Colton forgot his papers that he needs for a meeting. He asked me to come over here and pick them up. That was why I broke in to your house."

He kept eating like that information was irrelevant. "I don't care."

"You weren't a little alarmed to see me standing in your hallway?"

"I was only alarmed because you were fully clothed."

I wanted to roll my eyes but didn't. "You assumed I came here to sleep with you?"

"Yes. And it was hot as hell."

The only reason I came over was because I was told he wasn't here. But judging by the charged energy between us, this would have happened anyway. Whether it was here, at my apartment, or in the bathroom stall at a club, it would have transpired.

I kept eating, aware of the heaviness between my legs. "Thank you for dinner."

With both arms on the table, he kept eating. He looked up from time to time to stare at me, to give me that fierce gaze with the most beautiful eyes.

I didn't know what would happen now. We'd spent most of the evening fucking, so I should probably leave. I finished my plate then carried it to the sink. "I should get going. I've got to mail out those papers first thing in the morning."

He rose to his feet and looked at me coldly, like that was the wrong thing to say. "You aren't going anywhere."

"I'm not?" I asked, not really wanting to leave anyway. I had no idea what this was. I had no idea what this man wanted. But I didn't want to make the wrong decision and overstay my welcome. I didn't want the sex to stop. I would lose my mind if it did.

"No." He carried his plate to the counter and stood beside me. Tall, muscular, and smelling like sex, he was the most irresistible thing in the world. He could be on a calendar spread, a shirtless picture of him on every month of the year. "You're going to take off that shirt. Get in bed. Your ass will be up and your face will be down. When I'm done with these dishes, I'd better find you like that, come dripping down your thighs." He grabbed my neck and forced my gaze on his. "And I'm going to fuck your pussy until you scream."

WHEN I WOKE up the next morning, his face was next to mine on the pillow. His five-o'clock shadow had darkened through the night, and the outline of his jaw was less noticeable because of the hair that came through. When his eyes were closed and he was relaxed, he wasn't the hard and rugged man who barely said a few words.

He was Finn.

His arm was draped over my waist, and my leg was hiked over his hips. He was naked under the sheets, and his dick was hard with morning wood. Slowly, he breathed in and out, his powerful chest rising and falling with his rhythmic breathing.

I could stare at this man all day.

I knew I had to leave the comfortable bed because I had a shop to run. Now I wished I were an employee for someone else. That way, I could just bail and call in sick. But since I was the sole employee, all responsibility fell to my shoulders.

I slid out of bed and did my best not to wake him. I picked up my clothes off the floor and stuffed my old panties into the pocket of my jeans, going commando. I crept into the hallway then approached Colton's room.

That was the exact moment he called.

Just seeing his name on the screen made me feel guilty. I almost didn't answer.

I stepped inside his bedroom, found the folder sitting where he said it would be, and then took his call. "Hey...how's San Diego?"

"Jesus, what the hell have you been doing?"

I stilled beside his bed, the guilt gripping me by the throat. "Uh..."

"I kept trying to call you last night, but you didn't answer."

"Well, I—"

"Finn didn't answer either."

I was the worst liar in the world, so I didn't know what to say. All Colton had to do was think a little harder and our affair would be obvious. "You know how it is...work schedules get crazy." That didn't answer his question at all, but at least it was something. "Anyway, I have your papers, and I'm going to mail them right now."

"Really?" he asked. "One-day ship, right?"

"Yep. Got it."

"Phew. When you didn't pick up, I was afraid something bad happened."

Well...something very bad did happen. "Just chill,

Colt. I've got everything taken care of. And remember, you already got the job."

"But I can always be fired."

"You aren't going to be fired for forgetting some papers."

"But it's not a good first impression."

"Whatever. You're getting the papers, so it doesn't matter. Shoot me a text when you receive them."

"I will. So, everything good there?"

He just left yesterday, so I didn't know why we needed to make small talk. "Yeah, nothing new."

"Anything happen with Damon?"

Damon was the last person on my mind. The only guy I wanted was someone I finally had. "Haven't bumped into him. I've got to get to work, so I'll talk to you later, alright?"

"Yeah, sure. Thanks so much, Pepper." He hung up.

Thank god that was over. I gathered the folder then left the room, my jeans uncomfortable since I didn't have any panties on. All I had to do was get home, and then I could change.

I stepped back into the hallway and came face-to-face with Finn.

He stared at me like I'd done something wrong, like I had no right to leave the bed without his permission.

"I've got to get these mailed off before I head to work."

He maintained the same look, dark and hostile.

I stared at him and waited for him to say what was on his mind.

"You can leave when we're finished." He grabbed me by the elbow and dragged me back into the bedroom. "And we're nowhere near finished."

I STOOD at the counter in my shop the next day, constantly daydreaming since there were no customers to distract me. I did some paperwork, but my mind kept wandering back to the tattooed veteran who made my toes curl.

Jesus, I didn't know they made men like that.

He must have broken the heart of every woman he slept with. How could a woman have him then let him go? He was something else...something special. He was the best lover I'd ever had, so selfless and sexy.

I kept counting down the hours until I was released from this professional prison.

And back in the arms of the man I wanted so much.

I didn't even feel guilty about Colton. I was too happy to feel guilty.

It felt right with Finn. Like it should have been him all along.

The bell rang overhead when someone stepped

inside, and I snapped out of my thoughts to look at my new customer.

I must have been daydreaming too much, because the man who walked inside looked just like Finn. With tattoos peeking out from underneath his scrubs, he was sex on a stick. His stethoscope hung around his neck. This doctor could give me an exam anytime he wanted.

I blinked and realized it really was him.

Only one man in the world looked at me like that.

Instead of heading to the counter, he stopped and looked at the lingerie pieces on display. He admired a lacy black bodysuit with a snap crotch. So thin it was practically see-through, it was one of my racier pieces.

What the hell was he doing?

He walked to the counter and set it on top. It was my size. He opened his wallet and pulled out his card.

I stared at it for a moment before I raised my gaze to meet his. "What are you doing?"

"Buying something."

"Because...?"

"Do you interrogate all your customers like this?"

"No...but the men I'm sleeping with don't usually come in here and buy lingerie."

"This one does. Now ring me up."

I finally took his card and charged him for the expensive bodysuit. I put it in a bag with tissue paper then pushed it toward him across the counter.

He pushed it back. "I get off work at seven."

My heart started pounding in my chest when I realized what he'd done. The bodysuit was my size, and he wasn't buying it for anyone else. It was for me.

"This better be all you're wearing when I find you on my bed—waiting for me."

I STILL HAD his spare key, so I let myself in and put on the piece of lingerie he'd bought for me.

He was the only man ever to buy me lingerie.

It was such a turn-on to imagine a man walking into my store and picking out something he wanted to fuck his woman in. It was one of my fantasies, a fantasy that never came true. But then that sexy man walked in there looking like a hunk in his tattoos and scrubs and made my dream come true.

I put it on then waited on his bed. The mattress and sheets were so comfortable that it would be easy for me to fall asleep, but I was too aroused to drift off. I'd been pounded good and hard yesterday, but I was so horny, it seemed like that had never happened. I missed Finn. I missed his kisses, his touches, his gorgeous body... I missed everything.

Seven came and went, and he didn't walk through the door.

He seemed to always work late, so that didn't surprise me.

He was worth the wait.

When it turned eight thirty, my stomach growled in anger and forced me to go downstairs and raid his fridge. There was some leftover pizza, so I took out the box and ate at the counter. Standing in my slutty lingerie and pumps, I ate with my hair big and curled and makeup all over my face. My lipstick would smear, but I was too hungry to care.

My phone rang, and Colton's name appeared on the screen.

Normally, I would be happy to talk to him, but considering I was sneaking around behind his back, he just made me feel guilty. I answered because it would be suspicious if I didn't. "How was your first day?"

"Pretty good. I got the papers, by the way."

"Good. Now you can chill." I kept eating.

"Eating?"

"Of course."

"Pizza?"

I stilled, afraid he was watching me on a hidden camera. "How did you know that...?"

"Because it's your favorite," he teased. "And it sounds like you're tearing through the crust with your teeth."

He was dead on. "San Diego must be nice. Tell the sun I said hi. I can't remember the last time I saw it."

"I'll pass along the message."

"And how's the work so far?"

"I like it a lot, actually. I know I won't be working with these people, but everyone is nice and easy to talk to. Also, they're passionate about their work. We're going out for drinks in a little bit."

"That sounds like fun. I'll let you go."

"Whoa, hold on. Tell me about your day."

Well, Finn nearly made me come when he bought me lingerie at my own boutique. If only I could say that. "Well…" I heard the garage door open as Finn arrived. "You know, nothing interesting. Just work then went home to a pizza box." Now I wanted to get off the phone as quickly as possible without making it obvious that I was rushing.

The door opened, and he walked inside with his satchel. He stopped and stared at me, his eyes roaming over my long legs in my heels. He took in the sight of the lingerie, his eyes focused and hard. When he looked at my face, he seemed pissed I was on the phone.

"I should get going," I said as I watched Finn walk toward me. "My laundry is downstairs and—"

Finn snatched the phone out of my hand and ended the call.

"That was Colton—"

"I don't give a damn who it was." He slammed the phone down on the counter and pressed his chest against my back, his hands roaming over my curves in the thin material. He kissed my shoulder as his lips ran up to my neck. "What did I tell you?" His hand slid down my front and opened the crotch.

"I know...but I was hungry."

His fingers found my clit, and he rubbed the sensitive area with an experienced touch. "You disobeyed me."

I leaned my head back on his shoulder and felt the magic his fingers created. "I'm sorry..." I gripped his arm for balance and felt his cock pressed against my ass through his scrubs.

He cradled the back of my head with his hand as he kissed me, his fingers still rubbing my clit perfectly. His kiss was slow and sensual, just as it was when he was deep inside me. He chased away all my other concerns because he was the only thing that mattered.

My fingers found the drawstring on his bottoms, and I tugged on the string so it would come loose.

He kissed me harder and slipped two fingers inside me, moaning when he felt how damp I was. "Baby." He breathed into my mouth as he spoke, so much desire packed into that single word.

He could fuck me right against the counter I would be perfectly fine with that. We didn't need to make it upstairs.

His arms hooked behind my knees and back, and he lifted me to his chest. His lips found mine once again, and he kissed me as he carried me upstairs to his bedroom. When he dropped me on the bed, he shed all his clothes until he was down to his skin and ink.

My version of lingerie.

He moved on top of me and spread my legs with his thighs. His muscled mass weighed me down, and he slipped his hand into the back of my hair. His lips lowered to mine, and he kissed me as he slid inside, sinking nice and slow.

My legs locked around his waist, and I moaned into his mouth like I was having a climax then and there. "God...yes."

He sank until he was balls deep. A deep breath issued from his mouth, and he paused as he enjoyed me, like he'd forgotten how good it felt yesterday. His lips were immobile for just an instant before his kiss continued.

Then he started to move inside me.

I got lost in the lust and the desperation, the need and the desire. This man was all I wanted, all I needed. Anytime he was inside me, everything else in the world stopped. I couldn't think about anything else besides the two of us. "Finn..."

I DOZED off while he was in the shower, and his return

disturbed me from my nap. I watched him grab a fresh pair of boxers from his drawer and pull them up his chiseled legs before getting his sweatpants on.

This man was six foot three of perfection.

I was still in the slutty lingerie, the material riding up on my waist because the crotch was still unfastened. Stuffed with two loads of his come, I felt the weight sink toward my entrance and spread across my lips.

He sat at the edge of the bed and looked down at me. His blue eyes were naturally stoic, so it was difficult to read his thoughts. But when he was angry or focused, they were so expressive that his mood filled every corner of the room.

Every time I walked into his bedroom, it was perfectly maintained. The bed was made, the carpet was vacuumed, and his clothes were in his drawers or hanging in the closet. He didn't leave his dirty socks everywhere the way Colton did. And he didn't leave his shaver and toothbrush on the bathroom counter. This man was meticulous with his hygiene and overall cleanliness. That was a nice change. "I know I need to get dressed, but I'm just so comfortable..." There was something magical about this mattress and the ultra-soft sheets. His pillows had the perfect support. Not to mention, his bed smelled like the hottest man in the world.

"Why would you get dressed?" His hand moved

into my hair, and his thumb gently brushed the hair that started at my scalp. For a masculine man, he had the softest touch when he was in the mood to give it.

"I can't go home dressed like this." In my black lingerie and matching pumps. I would definitely get a free ride back home, but I would be harassed along the way. "I mean, I could. I'd definitely get a free dinner out of it."

"Why would you go home?" His hand moved to my neck next, his fingers lightly touching the skin.

"Because that's where I live…"

"Not this week." He rose from the bed and opened his drawer. He fished out a fresh t-shirt and a pair of boxers for me to wear. "And I'll get you that free meal." He tossed everything on the bed before he walked out.

I didn't want to go home anyway, but I didn't want to overstay my welcome either. But this week was our only opportunity to enjoy each other without Colton catching us. When this week was over, I suspected we would be over too. Might as well enjoy it as much as possible.

I joined him downstairs and had a real dinner. He whipped up chicken, rice, and vegetables, and then we worked together to clean the pots and pans along with the dishes. Once everything was finished, we sat on the couch together and watched the game.

Just like a couple.

With his knees apart and a scotch in one hand, his

other arm was wrapped around me as he held me into his body.

My face rested against his chest, and my arm was hooked around his muscular stomach. I didn't even care about the game because all I cared about was this beautiful man beside me. Being there with him was so inherently comfortable, I was surprised this didn't happen sooner. I got the best sex of my life, and when we were finished, we didn't need to fill the silence with conversation. Finn was a man of few words, the kind that could convey most of his feelings just through his stare.

When a commercial aired, I sat up and ran my fingers through my hair.

He drank his scotch then set the glass on the end table.

"I want to ask you something."

"Anything." He turned to me, his blue eyes innately intimidating because they were so powerful. His hand moved to my thigh, and he gave me his full attention, just the way he did when he was between my legs. He didn't make me feel like another conquest. He made me feel like a woman, a woman who belonged to him.

"Anything...that's a lot of things I could ask."

"I have nothing to hide."

He was quiet about his time in the military. When I asked him about it, he always deflected the question. It made me wonder if he would answer them now. But I didn't want to discuss something he was so uncomfortable talking about, so I didn't broach the subject. "Do you not wear condoms with a lot of women...?" When he refused to put on a condom the first time, I was too aroused to really fight it. I'd been on the same birth control my entire life, so I wasn't worried about getting pregnant. But this man was a known manwhore, so his dick had been everywhere. I should have been more responsible, but in hindsight, I was simply too deep in the situation.

His eyes shifted back and forth slightly as he absorbed the question. He didn't blink or turn away, continuing to face me head on. "No."

"No...as in you don't wear condoms?" The disappointment flooded through me. Finn seemed too intelligent to risk catching something from his lovers or knocking them up. There were tons of women who would want to get pregnant just so they could keep him in their lives forever.

"As in, I always wear a condom."

Instant relief.

"Except with you."

My eyes softened as I looked into his, both relieved and touched by the revelation. "Not once?"

He shook his head slightly. "Not even when I lost my virginity. My relationships are usually one-night stands. Sometimes, they last the weekend. But in every case, I don't know the women very well. We aren't friends, barely acquaintances. I can't trust someone I don't know."

"And that's why you didn't wear anything with me? Because you trust me?"

He was quiet as he looked into my eyes. He hadn't blinked once since the conversation began. "That's not the only reason." His fingers ran through my hair, pulling the soft strands away from my face. "You know that." Finn wasn't a romantic guy, but when he looked at me like that, he swept me off my feet.

I got lost in his eyes so easily. This man had captured my complete focus from the moment I met him. He wasn't just handsome, but the darkness of his soul gave him so much mystery. He was more mature than all the men I'd ever dated. He said little with his mouth, but everything else with his masculine presence. He was strong but not overbearing. He was manly but not possessive. And not to mention, he was a veteran...which automatically made him the sexiest guy ever.

What would have happened if I'd met Finn before Colton? Would I have married him instead? Would I be able to have an open relationship with the man who'd swept me off my feet? I didn't regret my marriage to Colton. But I did regret the situation we were currently in. "What are we going to do when Colton comes back?"

He continued to stare at me like he didn't register my question. "I'd rather worry about that later."

"It's only a few days away."

"And I'm not wasting those few days thinking about him." His fingers dug lightly into my thigh.

I didn't want to either. I wanted to stop time and enjoy every second until reality returned. "It's ironic that Jax was so insecure about Colton, when he should have been concerned about you..."

"Only weak men are jealous."

"You never get jealous?" I asked. "You weren't jealous when I was with Jax?"

"I didn't like you being with him because I wanted you for myself. That's not jealous. And it's ridiculous for a straight man to be jealous of a gay one. That shows he has a weak mind and a lack of confidence."

"Then I must have a weak mind...because I'm jealous every time a woman buys you a drink." I wanted to throw a tantrum right on the spot because I was so devastated. I hated seeing the way the women eyed him like a hot piece of ass, a hunk they wanted to take home.

His eyes narrowed slightly, like that response pleased him. "You were jealous because I wasn't yours. Now that I am, you have no reason to be jealous. I'll make every woman in the world jealous of you."

This guy had better lines than Romeo. I liked this soft version, a side he never showed anyone else. The game came back on, but neither one of us paid attention to it. I grabbed the front of his sweatpants and pushed them down, knowing there would be a hard dick waiting for me. I kicked off my bottoms then straddled his hips, my lips pressing against the thick length of his shaft. "I'll make them jealous myself."

11

PEPPER

The week passed in the blink of an eye.

I slept over every night and got used to the rhythmic sound of his deep breathing. His powerful heartbeat thumped against my palm as I snuggled into his side. It'd only been a few days, but now it felt like a lifetime.

Like I'd been sleeping with him all along.

I woke up that morning with disappointment in my heart. Colton would be arriving at the airport later that night, so our glorious week was over. I moved closer into Finn's side and refused to move, not wanting to give him up so easily.

It was a Saturday morning, and the rain pelted the windows. The light sound was so common that it never woke me up. Even when a bad storm hit, it didn't make me crack an eye. I snuggled into the tank beside me

and enjoyed sleeping in, loving the fact that I didn't
have to work that day.

Finn didn't either.

He rolled over in his sleep, turning toward me as
his chest slid past my hand. His arm immediately
hooked around my waist, and he buried his face in my
hair. He wasn't awake, but he seemed to be aware of my
presence.

I felt him lie against me, his hard dick against my
thigh.

I wished I could wake up like this every morning.

With a rock-hard, sexy guy on top of me who'd
thoroughly pleased me the night before. I didn't realize
there was such a thing as regular orgasms. With
Colton, it was usually hit or miss, and with Jax, the sex
was pretty good but nothing compared to this. Was
Finn just good in bed? Or was I just infatuated
with him?

He sighed quietly before he opened his eyes. It
took him a minute to focus on my gaze, to look into my
green eyes and realize I was right there with him. His
hand automatically slid up my back, and he kissed my
neck in greeting.

I loved waking up to this man.

He rolled on top of me, ready for sex right away. He
let his body sink into me more than usual, his weight
pressing me into the mattress. His face returned to my

neck as he slid his cock inside me, finding my entrance without even checking for it.

He started to thrust gently, still waking up as his cock slid deep inside my pussy.

My ankles locked together around his waist, and I moaned as he pressed my head into the pillow. My hands glided over his body, and I appreciated the feeling of this man. I pulled him closer to me and whispered his name over and over again. "Finn..." A man's name never felt more at home on my lips. I could whisper it forever, could admit that he owned my mind, body, and soul freely.

"Baby." He breathed against my neck, his lips lightly brushing against my skin.

I loved it when he called me that. I loved the possessiveness, the way he owned me. I never wanted to be owned more.

My toes started to curl as my climax approached. My nails anchored into his back as I held on for take-off. Maybe Finn wasn't that great in bed, but I was so aroused by him that he didn't need to do much to get me off. I was so deeply absorbed in this man that just having him inside me was enough. "Yes..."

He thrust harder as I climaxed, bringing himself to orgasm at the same time. His body shuddered as his cock thickened inside me with release. He moaned as he gave me another load to accompany the one he'd given me last night. He grunted before his cock started to soften.

That was a great way to start the morning.

He rolled off me then lay beside me, slightly out of breath from the lazy fuck he'd just given me. His eyes still possessed that sexy and sleepy look, like he hadn't fully woken up yet.

I propped myself up on one arm and looked down at him, my fingers trailing the grooves in his abs. I watched him blink a few times, my pussy full of the come he'd just given me. Staying in his beautiful house by the coast had been a dream, and I didn't want it to end. I never minded my apartment, but now it felt like a cage. "Sleep well?"

"I always sleep well with you."

"Do you not normally sleep well?" My hand rubbed his hard chest, my eyes taking in the ink on this skin. There were images of foreign places, probably locations where he was stationed during his service. His skin was an autobiographical canvas, a story of service, camaraderie, and death.

"No."

"Why is that?"

He stared at the ceiling, his eyes coming into focus now that he was fully awake. "Nightmares."

My hand stopped at the center of his chest. "Oh... what are your nightmares about?"

He took in the ceiling as he considered the question, his eyes gazing into a past only he could see. "War."

He never talked about his time in the military, but he seemed to be sharing it with me freely. "Did you see a lot of it?"

All he did was nod.

"I can't even imagine..."

"It's not as organized as film portrays it. It's loud, confusing, and even with all the technology we have, it's still chaotic. There isn't much time to make decisions. Everything happens in a split second. And those decisions have dire consequences...resulting in death. I lost a lot of good men in the field. Some of them were beyond saving. Others would have had a chance if they got to me sooner."

I started to rub his chest again, unable to fathom the gore he witnessed. Finn was calm and even-tempered, and sometimes I forgot what he'd been through. "I'm sorry..."

He finally turned his head and looked at me. "It's too early in the morning to talk about this stuff. Conversations like these should only happen with a scotch in hand."

"I didn't mean to pry..."

"I know, baby. You weren't." The backs of his fingers traced down my body, starting at my neck and descending between my tits.

"Will you ever talk about it with me?"

His eyes followed his fingers. Then he gave a slight nod.

"Can I ask about your tattoos?" My hand moved to his chest. "It looks like a story."

"It is a story. It's ten years of my life in the service." He pointed to the various military dog tags. "These are the friends I lost." He pointed to other images. "These are the places I was stationed. The rest of the ink is a collage of my memories."

"Not to seem insensitive, but...it's really sexy."

The corner of his mouth rose in a smile, a rare gesture from a guy like him. "I've been told that before."

He'd been told that a lot, I bet. "So...how many women have you been with?"

His smile slowly disappeared. "I hate that question."

"It's just a question."

"I have a better one." His fingers continued to caress my skin. "How many women have I slept with who meant something to me?" His fingers trailed back up to my neck as his eyes locked on mine. "One."

"One?" I asked. "You're in your thirties, and there's only been one woman?"

He nodded. "You know exactly who that woman is."

It was another romantic thing that made my knees grow weak. "Why won't you answer the first question?"

"I'll answer it. I just don't think it matters."

Since he seemed uncomfortable sharing it, I didn't press him on it. "Even when you were in the military, you didn't have relationships? Not with the female officers?"

"No. The only thing I cared about was serving, fucking, and drinking." He turned blunt once again, being exactly who he was without shame. "I never imagined I would ever meet a woman I actually liked, have feelings for someone that went beyond sex. I'm a difficult man to impress. But then this sexy brunette captured my notice the second I looked into her beautiful green eyes...and I cursed my brother for meeting you first."

I leaned down and pressed a kiss to one of his tattoos, a country in the far north of the region where he must have been stationed at some point in time. "He'll be home later tonight. What does that mean for us?" Would we be responsible and end this relationship before he returned? There was no way we could sneak around behind his back and not get caught. There was no hope for us. We should just treasure this week as a good memory, a way for us to get the urge out of our systems.

"What do you want, baby?" His arm wrapped around my waist, and he pulled me on top of him, his large size easily holding my weight.

I wanted Finn to be some random guy I met at a

bar, not my ex-husband's brother. I wanted nothing to stand in our way so we could enjoy each other as long as we wanted. "This can't last. Colton is so prominent in both of our lives that we'll get caught eventually. And that's the worst way he could find out."

He sighed quietly. "You're probably right."

"So maybe we should end this. We had the week to bang it out of our systems." The logical woman inside me knew it was the right decision. This had no future. If we were going to be together, we should talk to Colton because that would be better than if he found out some other way. But the woman who was stuffed with his come felt differently. She wanted to keep this going, wanted to sneak around because it would be even hotter that way.

"I could never bang you out of my system." His hand trailed down my back, his fingers tracing the curvature of my spine. "I've been with a lot of women, but none who compare to you."

"Well, if you've never been with a woman without a condom, I have an unfair advantage."

"It's not just that."

"Then what is it?" I whispered, finding him even more attractive when he was soft like this, showing his feelings without holding back. He was so rough and rugged all the time, but when it was just the two of us, he wore his heart on his sleeve. His transparency was even sexier than his masculine stoicism.

He studied my face as he considered his answer.

"I'm not the most beautiful woman in the world. I'm not the brightest or the most fun."

"Even if that were true, it doesn't matter. I can't explain the way I feel, even if I were better with words. I just feel a connection with you. I felt it the moment we met. You hadn't even opened your mouth to speak, and I still knew. Even when I thought you were still married to my brother, I felt it. Why? It's a mystery. Don't expect me to recite a poem about my emotions, not when I hardly understand the way I feel as it is."

His explanation didn't say much of anything, but it was still beautiful—coming from him. "So, we have a few hours left together. What should we do?" I didn't want to think about the pain I would feel once this was over. I would have to be grateful that it happened, to remember he'd been mine when I saw him with someone else. He would take her home and fuck her, but she would never compete with me.

His eyes narrowed with focus. "The thing we do best."

AFTER WE CLEANED up the house and erased all trace of my presence, Finn drove me to my apartment in the city. It was on the way to the airport, so it was right on his route.

He kept his eyes on the road and didn't make conversation.

There was nothing to talk about anyway. The radio was off, and the rain acted as the background noise. I watched the drops splatter against the windshield then be swiped away by the wipers.

This goodbye would be painful, but I had to be strong about it. The moment his lips were on mine, I knew our relationship was temporary. We had a one-night stand that lasted an entire week. I had no idea that it would be so magical, that I would want Finn even more by the time we were done.

He pulled over to the curb and turned off the engine. He sighed quietly then looked at his dashboard, his chin slightly tilted toward his chest. He didn't have a lot of time to linger because Colton's plane would be landing any second.

I didn't want to make this more difficult than necessary. "Friends?" I extended my right hand in the gesture of a handshake.

He lifted his gaze and looked at me, ignoring my extended hand. "I never want to be the kind of friends that shake hands."

"Alright..." I slowly lowered it. "What kind of friends do you want to be?"

He ignored me and got out of the truck, prepared to walk me to my door.

I grabbed my bag and walked with him into the

building, indifferent to the rain that flattened my hair. We made the long walk up the stairs and to my apartment door. Not once during that week had he come over. I hadn't even been at my apartment for more than a few minutes.

He stopped in front of me, failing to mask the pain on his face. "I don't want to be friends. But I don't know what else we can be." His arms circled my waist, and he hugged me, his arms tight around the small of my back.

I rested my cheek against his chest, trying to treasure the moment as much as possible. I loved this hard chest, this strong, beating heart. His scent was my new perfume. I didn't want to let this man go, to let him slip from my grasp into the arms of another lover.

His hand moved to the back of my neck, and he kissed my forehead. "I'll miss you, baby."

"I'll miss you too." I closed my eyes as I felt his lips on my forehead, the soft fullness that had kissed me everywhere so many times.

He abruptly released me and walked away, dismissing me the way usually did, without a backward glance. The muscles of his back moved fluidly as he carried himself down the hallway and out of sight.

It took me a second to let myself inside because the feeling of loss was so powerful. It'd only been a week of fucking and talking, but it was one of the best weeks of my life. When the sadness because too much, I reminded myself that I knew this was for the best. Even if Colton ever were to give his blessing, the relationship still didn't have a significant longevity. It was better to be hurt now when the pain wasn't excruciating, when I was still happy we got to enjoy each other at all.

12

COLTON

I spotted Finn's truck pulling up to the loading zone, so I tossed my suitcase in the space behind the seat and hopped inside. It was raining, like always, so we pulled onto the wet road and watched the pedestrians move down the sidewalks with their umbrellas.

I missed the California sun, but I was happy to be home. "Thanks for picking me up."

"Yeah, no problem." With one hand on the wheel, he looked out at the road with the same brooding stare he usually wore. But he seemed particularly moody that day, like the weather had squashed whatever joy he had. "Have a good trip?"

"Yeah, it was great. I worked a lot, but I also went out with my coworkers a lot. Time passed so quickly."

"Yeah...I know what you mean."

"You really enjoyed me being gone that much?" I asked incredulously.

"Actually, I did." He drove through the city then headed to his home near the coast.

"What did you do while I was gone?"

He shrugged. "Worked."

"I hope you didn't have sex on every piece of furniture in the living room." I imagined the second I was gone, Finn had had a sex party. He hadn't been bringing women around often, so maybe he waited until he had more privacy.

He shrugged again. "That may have happened..."

I cringed. "Why did I ask?"

"Good question. Hope you learned your lesson."

We pulled up to the house, parked in the driveway, and walked inside.

The house was exactly as I remembered it, meticulously clean and smelling like pine needles. I didn't want to carry my bag up the stairs so I leaned it against the wall before I raided his fridge. I grabbed a beer and twisted off the cap.

Finn tossed his keys on the counter then headed to the stairs. "I'm gonna hit the gym."

"On a Saturday night?" I asked incredulously. I stood at the counter and kept drinking my beer, shaking off the jitters from being on the plane for a few hours.

"Yep."

My brother was innately moody and quiet, but it seemed like there was something on his mind. He seemed down, like something disappointing had happened. "Finn?"

He turned around at the bottom of the staircase. "Hmm?"

"Everything alright?"

He looked me dead in the eye without showing a hint of emotion. "Yeah."

"You just seem a little down."

He turned back to the staircase. "You know me. I'm always a little bummed."

"So, did you take my advice?" I sat across from Zach in our favorite booth at the bar. We were both drinking light beer. When you drank as often as we did, you had to cut back at some point.

"With Stella?" He wore a t-shirt that stretched his arms and a backward baseball cap.

"Yeah."

"Kinda hard to do when she only wants me when Finn is around." He rolled his eyes then drank from his beer.

"Well, you'll run into Finn eventually. Make your move then."

"If she weren't so hot, I wouldn't put up with this. I've done a lot less for pussy."

"Then why are you bothering?"

He shrugged. "I've had a crush on her forever. I want her in whatever way I can."

"That's deep."

"Shut up." He grabbed a handful of peanuts from the bowl and threw them at me.

The shavings got all over my shirt, so I wiped the crumbs away. "Thanks for that..."

"Seen Tom yet?"

"I invited him to hang with us tonight."

"Really? Already introducing him to your friends?"

"I don't really see it that way. We're all hanging out, and I wanted him to join us. No big deal."

"I guess. But it seems like you really like the guy."

The guy had an eight-pack and a boyish smile. Tom was perfect. "Oh, I do. I don't want to rush it, but it's hard not to get carried away. I loved Pepper with my whole heart...but it was never anything like this. I hardly know the guy, and butterflies are soaring in my stomach. Sometimes I want to tell Pepper these things, but I feel too insensitive."

"Maybe when she settles down with someone."

"Yeah. I want her to be happy before I brag about being happy." My parents were right for being disappointed in me. Pepper was forgiving, but what I did to her was nearly unforgivable. Being gay wasn't a crime...but lying about it was.

"She's a beautiful woman, so that shouldn't be hard."

I narrowed my eyes at the comment.

"What?" he asked innocently. "It's not like I said she had a nice ass or something...even though she does."

"I'll dump this bowl of peanuts on your head." I grabbed the bowl and dragged it toward me.

"What?" he asked. "Last time I checked, she was a single woman, and you were with someone else. I can't check her out?"

"If I were straight, you know you would be crossing a line. Just because I'm gay doesn't mean she's not my ex, that the bro-code doesn't apply here. She's off-limits. If I catch you looking at her ass, I'll slam this bowl on your head."

He nodded slightly. "I guess that makes sense. But what I said still goes. It won't take her long to find someone. Look at what happened with Jax. All she tried to do was get laid, and that guy wanted to marry her."

"Doesn't surprise me." Pepper was the perfect woman. There were so many times I wished I were straight just to keep her. "Did you guys hang out while I was gone?"

He shook his head. "No, I didn't see her. I don't think the girls did either."

"I guess she was busy. Maybe she went on a date or something."

"Maybe," he said. "Like I said—"

"I'll shove these peanuts up your nose, asshole."

Pepper walked inside at that moment, wearing skinny black jeans, gray booties, and a long-sleeved top that highlighted her hourglass frame. Her hair was slightly curled at the ends because it had managed to survive the nonstop rain that afternoon. She grabbed a beer at the bar first before she joined us. "What happened to the peanuts?" There were crumbs spread out everywhere, like a child had been making a mess before we arrived.

"Colt kept trying to use them as a weapon," Zach explained.

"And why do you need a weapon?" she asked, looking at me.

"You know, because Zach is a little bitch." I drank my beer.

"Big bitch," Zach corrected. "I'm over six feet."

"Fine," I said as I rolled my eyes. "Big bitch."

Pepper chuckled. "So, is it good to be back home? To be pelted with rain constantly?"

"It is nice, actually," I said. "The heat gets old. It can be over a hundred degrees on most days in San Diego, even in November. It's crazy."

"Yuck." She made a disgusted face. "I'll take the

rain and the cold over heat any day. My skin can't stand direct sunlight for more than fifteen minutes."

"No wonder why you hated Hawaii for our honeymoon," I said with a chuckle.

"I didn't hate it," she corrected. "It was just so sunny all the time. There weren't even any clouds to break it up. It was hot, sunny, humid. A Seattle girl can only stand that climate for so long."

"I'm with her on that." Zach clinked his bottle against hers. "I love hiking, and there's no way I could hike when it's hot like that. I love hiking Mount Rainier when it's constantly drizzling. Keeps you cool."

I'd never been athletic like Zach. I liked to play basketball every now and then, but I didn't go out of my way to hike on a Saturday morning. "What did you do this week, Pepper?"

"Me?" she asked, like she was surprised by the question.

"Yeah," I said. "Zach said he didn't see you."

"Oh." She tapped her fingers against the side of her bottle. "I worked a lot. Got a lot of new inventory. Then I went home and ate a lot of pizza. Pretty uneventful, honestly."

"That does sound boring," I said. "Did you go on any dates?"

"Dates?" she asked incredulously. "Me? No." She laughed like the question was completely absurd.

"Nope, just stayed home...alone. By myself. The only date I had was with a pizza box."

She was oddly defensive, but I didn't press her on it. Maybe it was still awkward for her to talk about that stuff with me. We'd seemed to move past it, but maybe I was wrong. "When I came home, Finn seemed moody. Moodier than usual, at least."

"Why would I care about that?" she blurted. "I didn't see Finn while you were gone."

Zach turned to her, his eyebrow raised.

I raised an eyebrow too. "I didn't say you would. I'm just talking."

"Oh..." She nodded slowly. "Finn seems like a moody guy, so there's no surprise there."

"Did you talk to him while I was gone?" I asked.

"No," she barked. "I said that already."

"I just thought maybe you knew something." I picked up one of the peanuts off the table and cracked it open with my fingers. "He was quieter than usual. Seemed to want to be alone. When I asked what was wrong, he said there was nothing to worry about."

Pepper hung on my every word, staring at me with her fingers secured around her beer. "He's a veteran and a doctor. He probably has a lot on his mind that none of us could possibly understand."

"Yeah...that's true." My brother never talked about those things with me, but after everything he'd been through, he must struggle with stress on a daily basis, whether it was because of his past or because of his job in the ER.

After I drank from my beer, I spotted Finn step inside. Even though it was cold outside, he still rocked a t-shirt and jeans like the temperature didn't affect him at all. He scanned the bar before he noticed me sitting with Pepper and Zach.

His eyes went to Pepper next. And that's where they stayed.

He arrived at the table, his quiet presence louder than the TVs in the corner. "Hey."

Pepper stared at him, her fingers resting against her bottle. She almost didn't say anything back, like she was in a trance. "Hey..."

The eye contact lasted a while.

Finn was the first one to turn away. "I'm gonna get a drink." He left the table and headed to the bar.

Pepper's eyes followed him the whole way.

"Are you checking out my brother?" I asked, seeing the way her eyes zoned in on his ass.

She instantly snapped out of it and turned her focus back to us. "So I can't check out your brother, but you could check out a bunch of guys when we were married?"

"Whoa...ouch." I raised both of my hands in defense. "You've been holding that ammunition for a while, huh?"

"Maybe a little," she said.

"Why do you hate it when everyone checks out everyone else?" Zach asked. "I compliment Pepper, and you're threatening to kill me with peanuts. Then she glances at Finn, who is super-hot, by the way, and you lose your shit again. Dude, chill."

"Okay...there's a lot of things wrong with that sentence," I said. "One, you think my brother is hot?"

Pepper looked at Zach, grinning widely.

"I don't personally find him attractive, alright?" Zach brushed off the suggestion by moving his hand around. "But I understand what the chicks see in him." He started counting off the reasons on his fingers. "One, the guy is tall. Two, the guy is ripped. Three, he's got tattoos. And not just any tattoos, but ink that shows his time in the service. Four, he's a veteran. Five, he's a doctor. Come on, the guy is the perfect catch, and you can't hold it against Pepper for looking. She's not gay."

Pepper clinked her beer against his. "I second all of that."

"Sorry," I said. "I guess it's just weird for me. He's always been the favorite of the family, and I guess I'm a little insecure about it."

"Well, Pepper already proved that she thinks you're hot," Zach said. "She married you. So there's no competition."

"Very true," Pepper said. "It shouldn't be a big deal if I think your brother is hot."

"Yeah." I realized I overreacted. Sometimes, I got

jealous when it came to Pepper. She wasn't my wife anymore, but I still felt like she was mine. My brother could have anything he wanted, but she was the one thing off-limits. If they ever got together, it would ruin my relationship with my brother and destroy my friendship with Pepper. But my paranoia was ridiculous because neither one of them would do that to me. "You're right. It's not like anything would ever happen. You guys wouldn't do that to me."

Pepper took a long drink of her beer, downing the rest of the contents even though she only sat down ten minutes ago.

Finn returned with his glass of scotch and placed a beer in front of Pepper. "It seemed like you were getting low." He scooted into the seat beside me, forcing me to slide toward the wall.

Now that we were all together, it turned quiet.

Finn drank from his glass and looked at the TV, not making eye contact with anyone. A distinct quietness settled over the table, making the moment somehow heavy. He cradled his glass close to his body and didn't seem to be in a talkative mood, even though he'd come out to socialize.

"How was work?" I asked, breaking the tension that seemed to come from nowhere.

He shrugged. "Long day. I'll leave it at that."

"Something happen?" Pepper asked.

He didn't turn his head, but his eyes shifted toward

her. "I had a critical patient. I stabilized him, but I doubt he's going to make it."

I bowed my head, realizing just how tough Finn had it. His entire adult life had been surrounded by death. He probably got paid well, but sadness hung on his conscience. "Sorry, man."

He shrugged before he looked at the TV again. "That's life."

"I'll buy you the next round," I said.

"Seems fair," Finn said. "Since you're the most expensive roommate I've ever had."

"Am not," I argued.

"When was the last time you picked up groceries?"

"I don't have a car," I argued.

"So, if you lived there alone, you would order pizza every day?" he asked incredulously. "No, you would make it work."

"Or you could let me take your truck," I suggested.

He chuckled before he brought the glass to his lips. "I'm not letting you anywhere near my truck. You don't even have a license."

"So?" I asked. "I still know how to drive."

"You don't have a license?" Zach asked in surprise.

I shrugged. "I never needed one, so I didn't bother. I have a passport for travel, but that's it."

"I don't have one either," Pepper said. "I walk to work every day, the grocery store is right around the block, and I couldn't afford a car anyway."

I turned to Finn. "If I get my license, will you let me borrow—"

"No." He drank from his glass again.

"Damn it," I said with a sigh.

"You look like you could use a double." A gorgeous brunette came to our table, appearing out of nowhere with a glass of scotch in her hand. She set it on the table beside Finn, her long brown hair pulled over one shoulder. She was in skinny jeans and a tight t-shirt, a storybook of ink covering both arms. It went all the way up her neck and down under the front of her shirt. She looked exactly Finn's type because she looked just like him.

Beautiful and covered in ink.

He looked up at her, and when he gave a slight smile in encouragement, it seemed like he knew her. "Thanks. I could use a triple."

She grabbed the glass he was holding and poured the remaining liquid into the double she'd brought. "Ta-da."

He chuckled. "Like magic." He brought the glass to his lips and took a drink. "Thank you."

With one hand on her hip, she kept smiling at him, falling under his spell like everyone else.

"Layla, let me introduce you." Finn turned to me. "This is my brother, Colton."

She smiled at me. "I see the similarities, but I

wouldn't have guessed you were brothers if I didn't know."

"Unfortunately, he didn't get the same quality DNA." He turned to Zach. "My friend, Zach."

"Pleasure." Layla smiled at him.

Zach couldn't stop staring at her busty chest.

Finn turned to Pepper last. "And this is my... friend...Pepper." He hesitated when he came to her, probably because he didn't know how to describe her. She was kinda his sister-in-law even though he'd never met her when we were actually married.

"Nice to meet you," Layla said.

"Yeah," Pepper said, forcing a smile that didn't seem genuine. "You too..."

Finn continued. "Layla works with me in the ER."

"Oh, so you're a nurse?" Zach asked.

"No," she said with a chuckle. "Doctor."

"Ooh..." Zach looked mortified when he realized he'd shoved his foot in his mouth with his sexist assumption. "Sorry, I—"

"It's cool," Layla said. "I get that a lot." She turned back to Finn. "Now, this guy is one hell of a doctor. He handles trauma without breaking a sweat. One guy came in with three gunshot wounds, and Finn practically looked bored. This guy can handle anything."

Finn remained humble, like always. "You're a great doctor too, Layla."

She smiled. "And he's so polite."

"Finn?" I asked incredulously. "The only time I hear him be polite is when he's talking to Mom."

"Aww." Layla's eyes turned affectionate. "Retired veteran who loves his momma. Man, that's hot." There wasn't a hint of sarcasm in her voice, and she didn't mind hitting on him right in front of us.

Finn brushed off her comment like it meant nothing to him. "Working tomorrow?"

"Morning shift. You?"

"Afternoon," he answered. "Looks like we'll cross paths."

"I hope so." She grabbed his forearm as it rested on the table. After a gentle squeeze, she walked away. "Enjoy your booze. You earned it."

Finn didn't turn around to watch her walk away. He didn't drink from the glass either.

Pepper drank her beer then stared at her bottle, like the scene was boring to her.

I couldn't believe my brother got hit on like that—left and right. He got offered more pussy than he could handle, and it wasn't just ordinary pussy. All the women were always beautiful, confident, and sexy. I never had that kind of luck—with men or women.

"Man, she definitely wants to fuck you," Zach said. "Like, bad."

Finn didn't respond. Like he hadn't heard what Zach said, he watched the game on the TV.

"Or did you already fuck her, and now she wants you to fuck her again?" Zach asked.

Finn gave an answer, which was surprising. "No."

"No?" I asked in surprise. "Really? How long have you been working with her?"

"Since I started." Finn still seemed bored by this conversation.

"Well, are you going to hit that?" Zach asked. "She's gorgeous. And with all that ink and that sexy body... Jesus."

"Maybe you should go for it," Finn asked. "She's single. She's mentioned it several times."

"Like I could get a woman like that," Zach said incredulously. "I'm a good-looking guy, but she's crazy-hot. And she's a doctor...damn. That's like the hottest chick I've ever seen."

"Enough," Pepper. "Let's stop objectifying the woman."

"Why?" Zach asked. "You've never cared about that before."

"She's Finn's friend," she said as she stared at her beer. "Maybe show some respect."

Zach rolled his eyes. "I don't think Finn cares, not when she'll be his fuck buddy soon."

Pepper ran her fingers through her hair, like she was warm on a summer day. Her skin turned slightly pink as the sweat started to form.

"I won't sleep with her." Finn announced it to the table.

"Why the hell not?" Zach asked. "What's wrong with her?"

"Nothing," Finn answered. "I'm not picky when it comes to women. But I don't sleep with my coworkers."

Pepper released a deep sigh.

"But you've brought nurses home before," I countered. "Remember the girl who walked around naked?"

"I remember," Finn said. "And that's fine. I don't work side by side with them. But another doctor would just create an uncomfortable situation. When I'm at work, I don't have time to focus on anything else besides my patients. A colleague who's pissed that I dumped them could make my life difficult."

"I guess that makes sense," Zach said. "But she's sooo hot—"

"Stella just walked in." I spotted her walk through the front door. "Remember what we talked about. You gotta be strong, alright?" Finn was right beside me, so Stella would revert to her usual behavior of doing whatever was necessary to make him jealous...even though it was totally pointless.

"Alright." Zach took a long drink of his beer, like he was taking a shot.

Stella came to the table. "Hey, guys. How's it going?" She turned to me. "How was your thingy?"

"Good," I said. "San Diego is really—"

"Honey, could you get up?" Stella asked Pepper. "So I can scoot in?"

Pepper didn't roll her eyes even though she obviously wanted to. She rose to her feet and let Stella slide in first. "Sure."

Stella took the seat beside Zach, and just like I expected, she was all over him. She wrapped her arm around his neck and leaned in to kiss him. "I missed you."

Zach had the strength to pull her arm off him. "No thanks." He turned his lips away from her kiss and grabbed his beer. Like she meant nothing to him, he took a drink and looked at one of the TVs on the other side of the bar.

I would never forget the look on Stella's face. She looked wounded—seriously wounded.

She stared at him with an open mouth, like she didn't know what to say to this betrayal. She must have been mortified because she wouldn't make eye contact with anyone.

Then it got awkward...super awkward.

13

PEPPER

Stella talked my ear off as we walked down the hallway to my apartment.

"Can you believe him?" she asked incredulously. "He just drops me like I'm nothing?"

I barely listened to what she said because all I could think about was Layla, the sexy goddess covered in bright ink who also had a license to practice medicine. She was so undeniably beautiful, so exotic, and I died inside when I watched her squeeze Finn's arm before she walked away.

Died.

I was just an ordinary brunette who sold sex clothes for a living.

I couldn't compete with that.

Finn said he wouldn't sleep with her, but that wouldn't last forever. That woman was way too beautiful to ignore. She would probably switch hospitals just so she could fuck him.

That's what I would do.

"I can't believe Zach." Stella stepped inside when I got the door unlocked. "Can you believe him?"

There was no way Finn didn't want to fuck Layla. She was exactly his type, a badass woman who loved ink as much as he did—and she looked amazing in it.

"Pepper? Are you listening?"

I snapped back to the conversation. "No offense, Stella, but you do the exact same thing to him."

Both of her hands went to her hips, a warning of the fire that was about to flare up. "Excuse me?"

"You pick him up when it's convenient, then drop him again. It's the exact same thing. You're just using him to make Finn jealous, and he knows that. How do you think that makes him feel?"

Her mouth stayed open because she was speechless.

"Yes, it was embarrassing, but I don't blame him. You forget that Zach is your friend, and you shouldn't take advantage of his feelings."

Her arms slowly crossed over her chest, and her mouth closed.

"I know you don't want to hear that, but he's my friend too. I know Finn hurt you, but that doesn't give you the right to hurt Zach."

She sighed slowly. "Yeah...I guess you're right."

"Why do you care so much about Finn anyway?" I asked. "I've never seen you so affected by someone else's opinion." Stella had always been confident and self-assured. She went for what she wanted and didn't care what the haters had to say. This was unlike her.

"I don't know... I've never been rejected before."

I had to stop myself from rolling my eyes. I'd been shot down a few times in my life, but I didn't let it bother me because it was normal. But knowing Stella had never experienced that once in her life because she was so breathtaking made me want to pull out that pretty hair.

"I guess he hurt my ego, and I couldn't let it go. I wanted to change his mind to prove something to myself."

"Prove what?" I grabbed a bottle of wine and poured two glasses. "That you're gorgeous? Stella, the world knows you're gorgeous. You have the perfect face, perfect hair, perfect body...you have the perfect everything. There's nothing to prove. Finn is just...I don't know." I had no idea why he turned her down because I never asked. "You shouldn't let a man's opinion change your confidence."

"Yeah...you're right." She grabbed the glass of wine off the counter and took a drink. "I should let it go."

"Definitely." When I drank from my glass, the color remaining from my lipstick smeared against the surface. "What about Zach?"

"What about him?"

"Why don't you go for him?"

She shook her head. "I don't know..."

"I doubt you only kissed him to make Finn jealous. If you don't want to kiss someone, you don't kiss them. Besides, he's good-looking, has a good job, he likes to be active...he's a catch. He may not be a bad boy like what you're used to, but he's still got potential."

"Yeah, maybe," she said. "But I'm pretty sure I blew it when I acted like that."

"You could start with an apology and see where it goes."

"Not a bad idea." She depleted the glass then set it on the counter. "I wasn't a very good friend to him, so it's the right thing to do, even if I still don't get that D."

I missed getting D from Finn. It'd only been a few days, but I missed it like crazy. What I missed the most was feeling his arms around me while we lay in bed. I missed his hard chest, his masculine smell, and the way he always touched my neck with those rough fingertips. So it wasn't even the sex I missed most...just him.

"So what about you?"

I stopped thinking about Finn and focused my gaze on her face. "What do you mean?"

"Are you getting D from anyone new?"

It felt strange to have these feelings for Finn and not be able to express them. I normally told Stella everything about my life. It didn't matter how embarrassing it was. She never laughed at me, unless she was laughing with me. "No. But I'm sure it'll happen soon."

"Definitely. When we go out this weekend, guys will be fighting each other to buy you a drink."

I'd never had a guy throw himself at me the way Layla threw herself at Finn. I was so jealous it hurt, but I had no right to feel that way. He wasn't mine. He was only mine for the week, but our time together was over. I didn't have any hold on him. So I should go out and move on with my life...even though that was the last thing I wanted to do. "Sounds like a plan."

After Stella and I had a few glasses of wine, she went home. I sat on the couch with the TV on and considered opening another bottle of wine, but if I continued to drink like that, I wouldn't be able to get my pants on. One, they wouldn't fit. And two, I would be too drunk to get them on anyway.

The one person I confided all my feelings to was the one person I couldn't tell. Colton got upset just watching me check out Finn. When he realized he'd overreacted, he'd said it was a stupid reaction because he knew we would never betray him like that.

Even though we already did.

My phone lit up with a text message. I looked at the screen and saw Finn's name. *I'm sorry about tonight.*

I knew he was referring to Layla persistently trying to get in his pants, something he had no control over.

She was just one of many women who touched his arm like that on a daily basis. It was something he shouldn't apologize for. *There's nothing to be sorry for.*

The last thing I want to do is hurt you.

And just like that, this man turned me into a puddle of feelings all over again. He made me want him more, not less. He made me want to grip tighter and never let him go. *I know. But I'm going to have to get used to it.*

I'll never get used to seeing you with someone else. But I'll try.

14

COLTON

After I woke up that morning, I went downstairs and made myself a bowl of cereal. I sat across from Finn, who was already awake and clean from a shower. Shirtless, he drank his morning coffee while he looked through the medical records he had to dictate.

I drank my coffee and waited for the caffeine to kick in on my system.

"How was your night?" Finn didn't look up from his computer as he spoke to me, his ink covering all the individual muscles of his chest and arms.

"Great." Tom had slept over...but we didn't get much sleep. "Yours?"

He shrugged and never answered.

"Do you work today?"

"Day shift."

"Does it suck working at different times of the day?" I'd always had a job that was eight-to-five. I wasn't sure if I would like working random times and random days of the week.

"No. It's better than something repetitive and boring."

"So even if you could do the exact job during the morning shifts, you wouldn't want to?" I asked in surprise.

"No. Different shifts bring in different kinds of patients. It's good to change things up."

"I guess that makes sense."

He grabbed his mug and took a drink.

"So, anything gonna happen with Layla?"

He finally lifted his chin to look at me. "I told you, I don't fuck my colleagues."

"Yeah, but, come on." I was gay, and I knew she was hot as hell. "Layla is insanely sexy. She's just like you. She's fit, covered in tattoos, she practices the same kind of medicine—"

"I don't want someone just like me."

"Well, if you don't want her, then maybe you're gay too."

His eyes narrowed. "Just because I don't want to fuck someone doesn't mean I'm gay."

"I meant it as a joke. I'm just shocked that someone like you wouldn't go for it. You never stick to the rules."

He didn't have a response to that.

"I just can't believe someone that gorgeous bought you a drink and you're immune to her charms. It's like you have some kind of superpower. Maybe you just get hit on all the time, so you're used to it."

"Maybe I'm difficult to impress."

"You just said the other night that you aren't picky when it comes to women."

"I'm not. But I am picky when it comes to professionalism."

"So if she worked somewhere else, would you fuck her?"

He never answered the question. "Why are you interested in who I fuck?"

I shrugged. "Because I'm your brother, and we talk about this stuff. Seems like you haven't been with anyone in a while, like you're going through a dry spell or something."

"Thanks for being so concerned about my dick..." His tone dripped sarcasm.

"I'm just curious. We're friends, right?"

He turned back to his computer.

Tom came down the stairs, dressed and ready for work. "Hey, Colt."

"Hey." I turned in my chair to look at him. "Sleep well?"

"Absolutely." He leaned down and kissed me. Then he laid eyes on my shirtless brother. "Whoa..."

Finn wasn't rude to him the way he was to me. He

looked up from his computer without a threatening gaze in his eyes. "Morning, Tom. There's coffee in the kitchen and some leftover eggs in the pan."

"Thanks, but I've got to get to work."

"I'll walk you out." I walked Tom to the front door then said goodbye on the porch.

"Do you realize how hot your brother is?" he asked, lowering his voice.

"Yes...I get that a lot." I rolled my eyes.

"Don't worry, he's not as hot as you." He kissed me on the mouth before he walked to his car parked at the curb. He waved before he drove away.

I returned to the kitchen. "You're a lot nicer to him than you are to me."

"Because he doesn't grill me about my sex life. And he has a car, so I don't have to drive you around."

"You didn't drive me around much in the first place."

"But I don't drive you around now at all."

"You don't mind driving Pepper home all the time," I countered.

"Because I actually like her." He turned to his computer then pulled out the first folder he would be dictating. "A lot more than you."

ZACH DRIBBLED the ball to the hoop and made the shot.

The ball tapped against the rim a few times before it finally sank inside. "Dude, this is so sick. I want to buy a house someday just to have a hoop."

"Yeah, it's nice." I grabbed the ball then dribbled back until I could make a three-pointer. "My brother doesn't use it much."

"That's a waste. He doesn't use this hoop, and he doesn't fuck Layla. What the hell is wrong with that guy?"

I shrugged then made the shot. "Beats me. I'll never understand that guy. So, have you talked to Stella?"

"Nope." He stood with his hands on his hips. "Haven't heard from her."

"I think you made the right decision."

"Yeah...or I just pissed her off."

"And that was the right decision." I passed the ball to him.

He chuckled then made the shot. "I guess it doesn't matter anyway. She was never going to sleep with me —unless Finn was sitting at the foot of the bed."

I shrugged. "If you still got to fuck her, I guess it wouldn't be so bad."

He shook his head as he laughed. "I'm not that desperate, man."

Finn's truck pulled into the driveway, so we both stepped aside to let him pull into the garage. That's when I noticed a large kennel in the bed of the truck. "Why does he have a kennel?"

"Did he get a dog?" Zach asked excitedly.

Finn got out of the truck, opened the bed, and then opened the door to the cage. "Come here, man."

"Oh my god, he got a dog!" Zach practically shrieked like a girl. "That's so sick."

A large German shepherd jumped to the ground then wagged his tail, looking at Finn like he was already bonded to his new owner. He was full-grown and already had an identification tag on.

"Who's this?" I kneeled down and gave him a good rubdown.

Zach did the same. "Wow, what a cool dog. What's his name?"

Finn closed the bed of the truck then looked down at both of us. "Soldier."

"Soldier?" I asked. "That's a pretty cool name."

"I didn't pick it. That's what his officer named him." Finn crossed his arms over his chest and watched us play with the new dog.

"The officer?" I stood up and looked at him.

"He's a K-9 dog. He's been working with the police for a long time. His handler came into the ER, we started talking, and he said that he's getting ready to retire. But since he's being relocated to the East Coast, he couldn't take him."

"So you took him?" I asked in surprise.

"Yep." Finn smiled as he looked down at his new

companion. "I've always wanted a dog, and I thought we would be a good fit for each other."

Soldier barked like he agreed.

A car pulled up to the curb, and both Pepper and Stella got out.

Zach glanced at Stella then turned back to me. "What's she doing here?"

I shrugged. "Pepper told me she was coming. Didn't mention Stella."

Pepper stopped in her tracks and threw her arms down. "Oh. My. God."

Stella jumped up and down. "It's a puppy!"

Soldier took off at a run and ran right toward Pepper. He leaned back on his hind legs and pawed at her chest, making a bark or two.

Finn commanded him with a bark of his own. "Soldier, down."

"Oh, he's fine." Pepper kneeled down and rubbed him everywhere, letting him lick her cheek. "Soldier, huh? You sound like a badass dog."

Soldier barked.

"He's so cute." Stella leaned down and scratched him behind the ears.

Finn stood with his arms over his chest, watching the girls play with his new dog.

"Damn," Zach said. "They're hogging the dog..."

"There will be plenty of time for you to play with him later," Finn said, amused.

Stella let Pepper have Soldier, and she walked right up to Zach, ignoring Finn and me like we weren't there. "I wanted to apologize for before. I was using you, and it was wrong. You're my friend, and that's not how friends treat each other."

It was a nice apology, but not exactly what Zach wanted to hear. He definitely didn't want to be her friend.

But he would be an ass if he didn't accept her apology. "Thanks for saying that. I forgive you."

"Wow." She crossed her arms over her chest. "You're forgiving."

He shrugged. "I'm not one to hold a grudge—especially against you."

She smiled, her eyes filling with affection. "Well, do you want to go out with me sometime?"

Zach almost did a double take, as if he couldn't believe what she'd just said. He looked at me then turned back to her. "Like, a *date* date? You know, where two people have a drink and then maybe grind up on each other against the door when they say goodnight? Or a drink between friends?"

She chuckled. "The first one. Is that a yes?"

"Uh, it's a hell yes."

I turned away from them and looked at Pepper, who had managed to rub Soldier so good he was lying on his side in the driveway with his eyes closed. His tongue hung out, and he looked like the happiest dog in the world.

Finn slowly walked toward her, his arms crossed. "Be careful. He'll like you more than me."

"Too late." She rubbed him behind the ears, which seemed to be his favorite spot. "He's so cute. Where did you find him?"

"He's a retired K-9 dog. I thought we would have a lot in common."

"That sounds perfect," she said. "You guys will get along so well."

"As long as you don't come between us," he teased.

She smiled at him. "I can't promise anything."

15

PEPPER

Stella and Zach left to go on their date, so I stayed in the living room with Soldier on my lap. He lay across me and continued to let me pet him, being the perfect, but also the heaviest, lap dog.

Finn sat on the other couch and watched us, a beer in his hand. "You're going to make him lazy."

"He's worked so hard all his life." Whenever I looked into those chocolate-covered eyes, I got so lost. He was the cutest dog ever. "He deserves to be pampered and coddled."

"That's not why I got him." Finn glanced at the TV from time to time, but he didn't seem to be watching it.

"Then why did you get him?" Colton asked. "To grab the paper from the doorstep every morning?"

"To jog with me," Finn said.

Colton lay on the couch with his feet resting on the other armrest. "I think you should use him to get laid. Judging by the way Pepper has been all over him, that dog is a chick magnet."

No. Finn was the chick magnet. "You could definitely get a lot of admirers jogging through the park with this guy."

"I don't want any admirers," Finn said automatically.

Colton's phone vibrated in his pocket, so he fished it out then stood up. "Tom is here. I'll see you guys later."

If Colton left, that meant I would be alone with Finn—in a house. That would not be good. "Where are you going?" When I stopped rubbing Soldier, he rubbed his nose against my hand so I would keep petting him.

Colton headed toward the front door. "I've got a hot date tonight. Don't wait up."

"Tonight?" I asked incredulously. "It's Thursday."

"So?" Colton asked with a raised eyebrow. "Everyone should get laid every night of the week."

"I second that." Finn raised his glass.

"See you later." Colton walked out and shut the door behind him.

When I came over here with Stella, I didn't anticipate being alone with Finn. But somehow, it worked out that way. Stella and Zach took off, and apparently,

Colton had a date with his new boyfriend, a relationship that seemed to be getting more serious by the day. This was a situation I hadn't anticipated.

The second Colton was gone, the heat cranked up to a sweltering degree. The tension was suffocating, and the distraction of the TV wasn't enough. I was very aware of how alone we were, how it was unlikely Colton would return anytime soon. That gave us all the privacy in the world. We could return to fucking like rabbits and coming all over each other.

Now it was all I could think about.

He turned and looked at me, as if he was thinking the same thing.

Whenever those blue eyes were on me, my throat went dry and my fingers numb. He made me feel so weak, made me forget the reason why we stopped fucking in the first place. Colton made it clear how much it would bother him if this happened. It was a bad idea—if I wanted to keep my best friend. "I should probably get going...getting late." I moved out of Soldier's way, then stood up.

Finn kept watching me. "I can drive you."

"No," I said quickly, knowing what would happen if he walked me to my door. I pulled out my phone and ordered an Uber.

Soldier moved to the floor and sat on the dog bed in front of the fireplace. He got comfortable and closed his eyes.

Finn hadn't looked back at the TV once.

"Don't look at me like that..."

"Like what?" His deep voice was so sexy, so much sexier when it was just the two of us and I could focus on it.

"You know."

"This is how I always look."

"But it's not how you look at everyone." I glanced at my phone and saw the driver was eight minutes away.

"You got me there." He took a drink of his beer then set it on the end table. He never looked back at the TV, choosing to look at me instead.

It was impossible to be alone with this man. My thoughts kept drifting to the sweaty memories of us together, our bodies climaxing and our moans echoing. My throat was parched, and my knees kept rubbing together. "I think I'm just going to wait outside..." I rose to my feet and walked past him toward the door.

He grabbed me by the leg and yanked me on top of him. "I miss you." His hand moved into my hair, and he pulled me close to him, our foreheads touching. "I miss you so fucking much."

"No..." I had to stay strong.

"Baby." He cupped my cheek and kissed me on the mouth.

I kissed him back automatically, because that was what my mouth desired most. But I pulled back and pressed against his chest. "He could walk in the door at any moment."

"I don't give a damn." He pushed down the front of his sweatpants and revealed his big and beautiful dick.

I looked at it and felt the withdrawals hit me. My vibrator was no match for what I missed most. My tongue swiped across my bottom lip automatically as I remembered how well he stretched me, how he made me feel like a goddess, not just a woman.

"One more time, baby."

I closed my eyes and tried to fight it, but I couldn't. I wanted this man so much, wanted to ride his dick just as I fantasized. I wanted to come all over him...over and over.

He grabbed my phone and canceled the Uber.

I looked at the thick vein in his dick and felt my resistance wane. Now I didn't care if Colton walked in and saw us. I wanted to push that thick crown past my lips and fuck him until my legs started to shake with exertion. I wanted to fuck him and make him forget about Layla, to feel like he belonged me to again.

I unbuttoned my jeans.

The second I caved, he ripped off my shirt and unclasped my bra. Then he helped me get my jeans off because he was too impatient to wait for me to do it myself. My jeans and panties were left on the floor while his boxers and sweatpants rested around his ankles.

My legs straddled his hips, and I pressed his thick crown to my entrance. With a subtle push and moans from us both, I slowly sank down, feeling that hot and hard dick stretch me wide apart.

He closed his eyes and squeezed both of my hips. "Fuck...this pussy." This man was strong and silent, but when he was fucking, he was easier to read than an open book. He didn't withhold his pleasure, making me feel like the sexiest thing in the world. His large hands gripped me tightly like he wouldn't let me leave no matter how hard I tried. I was his—I didn't have a choice in the matter.

My hands flattened against his chest, and I used his strong frame for balance. I could feel the heat from the fireplace against my back, vaguely hear the sound of the TV coming from behind me. If the front door opened at that moment, I probably wouldn't even notice it.

I slowly moved up and down, allowing my cunt to coat him with slickness. Once his dick was completely wet from tip to balls, my cream started to build up at the base of his length, my arousal so profound that this man would never need to lube up.

My fingers gently pressed into him as I stared at his handsome face, his clean jaw and those kissable lips. His eyes were the most stunning, so blue and beautiful. They didn't stare at me with his usual hardness. He gave me a special look no one else had the opportunity to see.

Not even Layla.

I knew I'd gotten myself into a bad situation when I didn't hop in that Uber. Better yet, I should have asked for a ride from Colton when I had the chance. No good could come of this. It would just make it harder to be around Finn. But my jealousy toward Layla had a lot to do with my weakness. I didn't want him to get so horny that he called her for the one-night stand she enthusiastically put on the table. I didn't want to share this man —even when he wasn't mine anymore. "Just tonight..."

He pushed his feet against the ground and thrust his hips against me. His hands kneaded my ass, and he kept thrusting his soaked cock inside me. "Tonight."

My ALARM WENT off the next morning, and I woke up beside Finn, his muscular frame taking up half the bed. He was on his side facing me, sexy as hell when his hair was messed up from my eager fingers.

Soldier lay at the foot of the bed, taking up almost as much space as his owner.

I grabbed my phone and turned off the alarm, immediately remembering what had happened last night. We had sex on the couch three times before we wound up in his bedroom. He carried me upstairs, fucked me one more time, and then made me pass out on his comfortable sheets.

I'd missed this bed.

I'd missed this man more.

Finn woke up at the sound of my movements, and he moved on top of me.

"I have to get to work..."

His legs separated mine, and he pinned my hands above my head. Even when he was half asleep, he was still the authoritative lover who made my legs throb with intensity. He tilted his hips and pressed his thick crown inside me, finding it with no effort. Then he slowly sank deep inside me.

And just like that, my resistance was gone.

He released my hands and kissed me, disregarding our morning breath. His tongue danced with mine as he kept thrusting inside me, sliding past the slickness that poured at his demand.

My arms locked around him, and I let him take me, let him own me. This man was so incredible in the sack that my body left my command and fell under his. I kissed him back as I felt him move deep inside me, bringing me to climax at lightning speed.

"Quiet, baby." His hand fisted my hair, and he thrust harder, doing his best to fuck me without tapping the headboard against the wall.

Staying quiet wasn't one of my strong suits, at least

not with Finn. My mouth moved into his neck, and I forced myself to be quiet, but what I shushed in my voice was amplified with my body. I bucked against him involuntarily, and my cunt gripped him with the strength of steel.

"Fuck." He sounded like he could feel it, feel the crushing force of my climaxing pussy. He gave his final pumps as I finished, then he came inside me, his dick throbbing as he finished.

If only every morning could be like that.

He rolled off me then closed his eyes again, as if he could fall back asleep.

I wished I could stay there and blow off my job. I wished I could spend the morning with him while Colton was at work. But I knew this was a one-time thing and I shouldn't get attached. Nothing had changed. But I did learn that I needed to avoid being alone with him at all costs...at least until we both really moved on.

I got out of bed and got dressed.

When Soldier realized it was time to wake up, he hopped off the bed and moved to the door, ready to go outside to do his business.

After a long sigh, Finn got out of bed. "I'll see if Colton is around." He pulled on his sweatpants and stepped out.

I sat on the edge of the bed and waited for the sound of noise. I couldn't even hear Finn's footsteps after he was downstairs, and if Colton was in his bedroom or the bathroom, he wasn't audible.

Minutes later, Finn returned. "I'll drive you home."

"You're certain he's not here?"

"Yep. I checked everywhere. Soldier couldn't find him either."

If a police dog couldn't find him, then he definitely wasn't in the house. "I'll call an Uber, then."

"Don't be stupid. I'll drive you."

"You don't have to—"

The look on his face was all he needed to shut me up.

"Alright..."

We went downstairs and spotted Soldier through the back window. He was running around on the grass, stretching his legs and getting his paws wet from the dew on the lawn.

"He loves it here," I said as I followed him to the kitchen.

"Yeah, he's a good dog. Obedient and quiet."

"And he's cute, affectionate, loving..."

He shrugged. "Those aren't the traits I'm looking for."

"Then why did you get him?" I countered.

He grabbed his wallet and keys off the counter.

"Because you thought he was cute," I said with victory. "Just admit it."

"Cute isn't in my vocabulary."

"You don't think I'm cute?" I asked, propping one hand on my hip.

He looked me in the eye as he pulled on his sweater and zipped it up. "No."

"No?" I asked, offended.

"Cute is the word you use to describe a litter of kittens. You're a full-grown woman, with sexy curves and perfect tits. You aren't even close to being cute."

I used to find the word complimentary, but Finn's opinion suddenly made me grateful that he didn't find me cute, that he found me to be the definition of sexy. Colton used to call me cute all the time. Now it was no wonder he turned out to be gay—because he'd never found me to be sexy. "That's—"

The front door opened and closed. "Coffee better be ready. I can barely keep my eyes open."

My eyes nearly popped out of my head as the terror gripped me by the chest. Instead of conversing in the kitchen, we should have left when we had the chance. Colton must have come home to get ready for work instead of bringing his clothes to Tom's place.

Finn kept his cool even though we were in some serious shit. He opened the door to the pantry then nodded for me to get inside.

I was glad he thought quickly on his feet because I had no idea where to hide. I stepped inside, and he shut the door behind me.

It was pitch-black inside, only lines of light coming through the cracks in the doorway.

Colton's feet grew louder as he entered the kitchen. "No coffee?"

It was amazing how calm Finn was. His brother had almost walked in and caught us sneaking around behind his back. That would be the most disturbing way for him to find out his brother was screwing his ex-wife. "Not yet. Was just about to make a pot."

"Got a late start?"

Finn poured the grounds into the maker, then flipped the button on the machine. "Getting used to Soldier."

"That dog is a chick magnet. When you take him for a jog through the park, women are gonna be stuck to you like glue...even though they already are."

Finn chose to be humble and didn't comment. "How was your night?"

"Awesome. I got a home-cooked meal and sex. What about you?"

"Pretty quiet night." The coffeemaker started to make the gurgling noises, and soon the coffee was dripping.

"When did Pepper leave?"

"A few minutes after you did. She took an Uber."

"I'm surprised you didn't drive her," he said sarcastically.

"She didn't want me to. So, are you going to work

today? Because you shouldn't be late when you're this new."

"We start an hour late today. Have a big meeting."

Ugh, that information would have been helpful yesterday.

Their conversation died away, and I assumed they both poured mugs of coffee.

I was already late to work, and now I wouldn't get the shop open for at least another hour. I would just walk out and face the consequences, but these were not the kind of consequences I wanted to face.

Colton's voice sounded from the dining table, which was out of sight of the garage door. "Work today?"

"Day shift." Finn's voice still sounded from the kitchen. "I'm going to head to the gym. I'll see you later."

I preferred to wait until Colton went upstairs, but if Finn was going for it now, I didn't have a choice. Colton might look in the pantry to make something to eat, so I couldn't stay there too long.

"Bye," Colton said.

Finn opened the pantry door and the garage door at the same time to mask the sound of both doors. Then he stepped aside so I could go first.

I darted into the garage like my life depended on it.

When we got into the truck, I lay flat with my head on his thigh just in case Colton came outside.

Finn grinned as he backed out of the garage. "I like this position." He hit the button on his visor to close the garage before he pulled onto the road and drove away.

After a few seconds, I sat up, the adrenaline pumping in my heart. "Oh my god, that was close."

He shrugged. "Colton is pretty clueless when it comes to his surroundings."

"But all he had to do was open the pantry door, and we would have been screwed."

"You give him too much credit." He kept brushing off the event like it wasn't a big deal.

But it was a big deal. "Finn, that could have been really bad."

"But it wasn't."

"Still..." This couldn't happen again. I would have felt terrible if Colton had opened the door and seen my horrified face. It would have only taken a few seconds for him to realize what happened, that his brother and best friend were getting it on behind his back—and we were lying to his face every day. "It can't happen again. That was the last time."

He kept his eyes on the road, one hand on the wheel. "Alright...the last time."

16

COLTON

"How'd it go with Stella?" I sat across from Zach in the booth at the bar. Finn left to get drinks, but he'd been gone while.

"Pretty good," he said. "She paid for the drinks, talked to me about work, and then she invited me to her place afterward."

"Whoa, you guys already slept together?" I knew Stella wasn't a shy woman, but since they were friends, that seemed a little fast.

"No. But we had a hot make-out session on her couch." He waggled his eyebrows.

"That's one hell of an apology." I looked over my shoulder and searched for Finn. "Where the hell is he? I need my beer."

Zach narrowed his eyes. "He's got two women fighting over him. God, he's such an asshole."

I saw two blondes standing with him at the bar, both wearing tight dresses and heels. With smiles plastered on their faces and gentle touches gracing his arm, they were both available and interested.

"Anytime that guy is out in public, he's getting pussy." Zach shook his head. "I should have gone into the military..."

"You wouldn't have been able to handle it." I turned back around and faced him. "Maybe I should just get my own beer from now on."

"I couldn't?" he asked incredulously. "To get hit on like that all the time, I'd definitely go to war."

I knew he was joking, but it was still insensitive. "Don't say things like that around Finn. It bothers him."

"Noted."

When I watched a group of girls walk inside, I recognized Pepper and her friends. Pepper wore a deep purple dress with black pumps, and Tatum and Stella looked just as eye-catching. They obviously had no idea we were there because they moved into a booth and kept talking.

"What?" Zach looked over his shoulder.

"Looks like they're having a girls' night."

He whistled quietly. "Stella is looking fine in that dress."

And Pepper wouldn't be single much longer looking like that.

"Should we go talk to them?" he asked.

I shrugged. "Maybe they want to do their own thing."

"Stella won't be doing her own thing dressed like that for long."

Finn finally returned from the bar with the beers. "Drink up."

"Took you long enough." I snatched my beer and scooted in so Finn would have room.

"Got sidetracked." He drank his beer then looked at the TV.

"You aren't going to hook up with them?" Zach asked incredulously. "They're two tens. That means they're a twenty."

Finn shrugged. "Just not in the mood."

"Not in the mood?" Zach couldn't comprehend the statement. "You're a young guy. You're always in the mood."

"It just gets old after a while. It may be a different partner, but it's always the same thing. No talking, just sex. It's the introduction, the same flirting. There's never anything interesting about them, we fuck, and then I have to deal with kicking them out."

Zach rolled his eyes. "I feel so bad for you..."

Pepper left the booth then strutted across the room, indifferent to our presence because she had no idea we were there. Her hips swayed back and forth, and heads turned in her direction. She had the perfect figure, gorgeous legs, a plump ass, and a narrow waist.

Finn was about to take a drink of his beer, but he slowly lowered it as she walked by, his neck craning as he stretched his ligaments to epic proportions. When she arrived at the bar, he completely pivoted in his seat just to look at her.

Zach whistled under his breath. "Your ex cleans up good."

I watched every man gawk at the woman who used to be my wife, even my own brother. But I couldn't get angry when she was single and gorgeous. That would be like screaming at the clouds every time it rained. It was pointless.

Finn scooted out of his seat. "Excuse me." He stood up and walked to the bar.

Zach watched him go. "Sometimes I wonder if Finn has a thing for Pepper."

"No. He wouldn't do that to me."

"Then why did he ditch us like that?"

I shrugged. "He's protective of her the way I am. Probably wants to make sure the guys don't bother her."

Zach stared at me for a few seconds before he took a drink. "Yeah...maybe that's it."

17

PEPPER

W hen I reached the bar, I ordered a vodka cranberry, something strong but also sweet. After the week I'd had, I needed something that would spike in my bloodstream. I was obsessed with a man I couldn't have, when I should be moving on with my life. Once I got a divorce, I was free to do whatever I wanted, but for some reason, I wanted to do stupid things.

Like sleep with my ex's brother.

There were a million guys out there. Why did I have to choose the one guy I couldn't have?

I was about to pay for the drinks when Finn appeared at my side, looking sexy as hell in his t-shirt that showed off his battle ink. A beer was in his hand, and he stood close to me like he was staking a claim in front of all the other guys at the bar. Since there was no man who could possibly compete with him, they steered clear.

When I smelled his scent and looked into those gorgeous eyes, my legs felt weak in my heels. He always took my breath away, stole it directly from my lungs. When the girls and I decided to go out tonight, I'd promised myself I'd at least try to meet someone new. But when Finn appeared out of nowhere, that made it impossible.

He stared at me without saying a word.

I didn't say anything back, as was customary.

The staring continued as the conversations erupted around us. The TV had a replay of the game, and the sound of glasses tapping against hard surfaces composed the background noise.

I gave in first. "Having a night out?"

"With Colt and Zach."

"Ooh...didn't see you."

"I definitely saw you." His eyes trailed down my body, looking at my curves in my skintight dress.

We'd agreed that we were finally over, but this scorching chemistry was impossible to ignore. Anytime we were alone together, it was rampant and hot, like we were standing right next to an inferno. I changed the subject to keep things safe. "I was hoping to meet someone tonight..."

"You can have any guy you want in here. They're all staring at us, wishing I would drop dead."

"You give me too much credit."

"And you don't give yourself enough." He stood close to me at the counter, so close that we looked like lovers more than friends.

"Because I'm not cute, right?"

He shook his head. "Not at all."

I turned back to my glass and took a drink.

"So, which guy do you like?"

"I don't know...I haven't even looked." How could I look, when the sexiest man in the world was right beside me?

"Do you even want to look?"

He already knew the answer to that. "You're making this harder than it needs to be."

"I find that unlikely. It can't be any harder."

He might be right about that. "How many women have made passes at you so far?"

He held his beer and stared at me.

"You aren't going to answer me?"

"I don't see why it matters."

"You're asking me which guy I want to hit on. You can't tell me who's hit on you?"

"That's because you don't want to hit on any of these guys," he said. "And I couldn't care less who's hit on me. They're always nothing compared to you. And

I'm afraid they'll always be nothing." He leaned his arm against the counter and stared at me, his powerful gaze burning through me with its intensity.

I came out here tonight with the intention of moving forward, not getting caught up in the sexual tension with this man. After hiding in the pantry, I realized I didn't want to be that person—a liar who snuck around. I felt like someone having an affair, sleazy and deceitful. It could be exciting at times, but mostly, I felt shady. "Finn, this needs to stop."

"It has stopped."

"No, it hasn't. We're fucking in the middle of this bar right now—with our eyes." We weren't touching, but that didn't mean we weren't wrapped up in each other. The room felt empty because we were the only people inside. This connection made us block out everything else but each other. It wasn't healthy, not when this would never have a future. "You should go home with someone, and so should I. This is never going to work, so we need to start acting like friends... real friends." I grabbed all the drinks and prepared to carry them back to the girls. "Don't make this harder on me than it needs to be. It's the first time in my life where I've found a man who actually feels right for me...but I can't have you. I'm not going to torture myself anymore. I don't want you to torture me either."

His eyes narrowed slightly, the sadness heavy in his gaze. He didn't reply to my comment, maybe because my admission made him uncomfortable. Maybe that was the key to putting distance between us—by putting my heart on my sleeve.

I grabbed the drinks and walked away. "Goodnight, Finn."

I WALKED in the door at midnight.

I slipped off my heels right away, tossed my clutch on the table, and then sat on the couch with my dress almost up to my waist. I should have gone into the bathroom to wash the makeup off my face, but I was too bummed to care about skin care.

My plan was to meet someone tonight, even if it was just for the evening, but Finn's appearance unnerved me. It reminded me there was only one man I truly wanted, a man I wanted even more than I ever had wanted my own husband. When we moved together, it was perfect, like the best sex in the world on drugs.

He was my drug.

But he wasn't an option. Even if he were, he never wanted to get married or have kids, so it wouldn't go anywhere anyway. He was just a heartbreaker who distracted me from the path I was meant to walk.

I shouldn't have slept with him in the first place.

Now we would never be friends.

But then again, were we ever really friends?

My eyes closed as I sat on the couch. I should get up and go to bed, but I was too tired to move. It was easier just to lie there, to let the exhaustion creep into my veins like an intravenous drug.

Another option would be to bust out my vibrator and think about the man I couldn't have, but that would only lead to self-loathing when I was finished. My fantasies never compared to reality anyway.

Just when I was about to get up, there was a knock on the door.

I rose to my feet and stared at the entryway, immediately assuming Finn was on the other side. There was no reason for Colton to stop by at this time of night without warning, and I doubted it would be my new neighbor across the hall.

I peeked through the peephole and saw Finn's handsome face looking back at me, unafraid to stare down the hole in the door. His eyes possessed that fire he usually wore when he was inside me. His intentions were obvious, even with a solid piece of wood in between us.

If I didn't want this to happen, I should just walk away and pretend I was asleep.

But I did want this. I wanted this man for more than just sex. I wanted him because he chased away the loneliness, made me feel sexy when I doubted my appearance. He reminded me that I was worth something, even if my husband left me for other men.

I unlocked the door and opened it.

He hadn't blinked since he knocked, and he continued that fierce stare now. With his muscular arms resting by his sides, he stood six foot three of pure masculine perfection. His strong chest rose and fell slowly with his breathing, and without expressing his desires verbally, he expressed them physically.

I knew it was a bad idea to open that door, but I did it anyway.

I had no chance against this man.

He allowed himself inside, crossed the threshold, and then dug his hand into my hair as he kissed me. His leg kicked the door shut behind him, and he gave me a searing kiss that made me forget all my doubts.

He made me forget everything.

His hand gripped the back of my dress and slowly bunched it up my waist, making my ass hang out in the seamless thong. One large hand gripped both cheeks as it made a bridge over my crack. His kiss continued at the same time, devouring me like a man should consume a woman.

A man had never kissed me like this, had never handled me with so much desire. Finn had had more partners than anyone I knew, but he made me feel like I was the only one who mattered, the only one who could make him as hard as steel.

My hands snaked under his shirt and felt the powerful abs of his body, the grooves that were so hard they could break a nail. I worshiped him with my fingertips, slowly pushing the shirt over his head and revealing his chiseled physique.

He grabbed the front of my dress and yanked it down, causing my tits to pop out the top.

My fingers undid his jeans and pushed them to his thighs.

Like it was the first time we'd ever been together, we yanked on each other's clothes and feasted on flesh.

He pushed me back to the bedroom, his jeans and boxers slipping to his ankles as his cock pressed against my stomach. He kept kissing me until we reached the foot of the bed in my bedroom.

He turned me around and lifted me onto the bed so I was on all fours. Then he grabbed the back of my neck and pushed it against the sheets, making my ass pop high into the air. He yanked my dress to my waist and pushed my panties to my knees.

His hand guided his cock to my entrance. He slowly pushed past my lips and sank inside me, collecting all the slickness as he entered as deep as he could go. Once he was fully sheathed and wet, he gripped my hips and fucked me hard.

Fucked me like a whore.

His hand flattened against my lower back, and he kept me in place as he slammed his dick deep inside me, moaning and grunting as he fucked my pussy like it belonged to him.

I moaned into the comforter, my hands reaching between my legs to grip the insides of his thighs.

"I'm the only man who fucks this pussy," he spoke as he jackhammered me, pounding me so hard, it actually hurt a little bit. His long cock kept hitting me deep, tapping me all the way to my cervix. "You understand me?"

Logic didn't matter anymore. I could keep fighting to restrain myself, but I'd already lost that battle a million times. Maybe it was wrong, but it didn't change the truth. Finn and I were together. We were going to stay together and keep fucking like this—for better or worse. "Yes."

He thrust hard inside me, making my body jerk. "Say it again."

"Yes."

"Yes, what?"

I was completely at his mercy, unable to fight the fire that ignited us both. "You're the only man who fucks this pussy."

THERE WAS something innately comforting in defeat. All the stress disappeared because it didn't seem to matter. I did my best to do the right thing, but that never seemed to work. Finn crossed the line so many times, and I didn't bother fighting him anymore.

I just accepted it.

We lay together in the darkness of my bedroom, my leg hooked around his hips, while his arm draped over my waist. Face-to-face, we stared at each other while the night deepened into morning.

It was almost four a.m.

We didn't spend time talking about what just happened or the fact that we'd chosen a path that would end terribly for both of us. We entertained ourselves with silent stares, with fucking and lovemaking.

He'd been staring at me for a while, showing no signs of fatigue.

My fingers moved to his chest, feeling the military dog tags that constantly adorned his hard body. "You never take these off?"

He shook his head slightly. "Never."

"May I ask why?" My fingers felt the hard metal of the tags, seeing his name engraved in the material.

"You can ask anything, baby." His hand glided across my back until he reached my hip. His fingers dug into the skin lightly, the touch comfortable and warm. "I wore them every day for ten years. It's a habit I don't want to break."

"Do you ever think about going back?"

He took a long time to consider the answer before

voicing it. "Sometimes. But I think it wouldn't be in the best interest of my health. Like most people who serve more than four years in the military, you see things you can't see unsee...and they haunt you. If I'd stayed any longer, I would have gotten worse. And when you hit a certain point...there's no coming back."

He never talked about his mental issues, and he seemed perfectly fine on the outside. But it was impossible to tell what someone was truly feeling. Someone could laugh and be the life of the party, but also struggle with the biggest demons. "It's smart to understand when you've had enough and remove yourself from the situation. You served your country long enough."

He watched me in the darkness, his touch resting against my belly.

"Was there something that happened that made you leave?" When he first moved in with Colton, he'd seemed to carry great pain on his shoulders, as if something happened that made him walk away. "A specific event that was the last straw for you?"

He stayed quiet, as if he had no intention of answering my question.

He said he would answer any question I had, so I stayed patient. My hand released his chain, and I rubbed his chest, feeling his strong heartbeat underneath the tips of my fingers.

"The nice things about working in the ER is you

don't know any of your patients. I see them with calm objectivity. There are no feelings involved, so I can do my job and give them the best care possible. But in the field...I knew all my men. So every save and every loss was very personal. One of my close friends was hit by a grenade in battle. When they got him to me, there was nothing I could do. All I did was sit there with his blood all over me and watch him die. I lied and said he would be alright, just so he could die comforted." He broke eye contact, shifting his gaze to another point in my room. "That was the end for me. When my deployment ended, I was honorably discharged from the military. They tried to get me to re-sign by offering me a lot of money...but there was no amount of money that could make me change my mind."

When his heart ached, so did mine. I could feel his sorrow like it was being transferred directly to me. This man had sacrificed so much, and I hated the fact that it hurt him so deeply. It was impossible to serve the country without collecting scars—both physically and mentally. It was obvious that Finn couldn't tolerate any more, that he had the courage to admit when he'd had enough. "I'm so sorry." Those words felt so empty on my ears, but I meant them deeply. They were the words people uttered when they didn't know what else to say. I didn't know what to say either...but I was apologetic.

"Nothing to be sorry about."

"I'm sorry you had to go through that."

He shrugged. "Someone has to do it. If it weren't me, it would just be someone else. It's a shitty job, but someone has to do it."

"Have you considered therapy?"

"I did therapy for two weeks when I first moved in with Colton."

"I didn't know that..."

"I'm not dismissing therapy, but when you've seen things like that, you can never unsee them. You can never think about the past and feel good about it. It's just something you have to carry forever. They don't tell you that when you first enlist."

"Why did you enlist?"

He took a deep breath as his eyes shifted back to me. "You're curious."

"I've always been curious...but I thought you didn't want to talk about it."

His hand glided up my belly and between my tits. "I wanted to serve my country and become a doctor. When I took my aptitude test for the military, I had unusually high scores. They offered me an opportunity to get my medical license for free in exchange for ten years of service. It was the perfect setup—so I took it. I have no student loans, I saved up a lot of money, and it's easy for me to get a job anywhere because of my experience."

"Yeah...not bad."

"I don't have any regrets about my time in the service. But it would be a mistake if I went back."

"Yes, it would. It's time you enjoy civilian life."

"I guess. Sometimes I miss my boys."

"I'm sure they miss you too. Do you keep in touch?"

"Sometimes through texting and social media. But when you're in the field, communication is hard."

I ran my fingers down his stomach. "I think it's good that you're here so you can spend time with your family. Your parents are still here, but they won't be around forever. It's good that you spend time with Colton too. I feel like you two have reconnected."

His eyes dilated slightly at the mention of his brother. "What happened with your family? My mother mentioned you didn't have anyone, but she didn't tell me why."

"My mom got pregnant really young. She didn't want to raise a baby on her own, so she gave me up for adoption. I ended up being in the system for a long time and placed in foster homes. It just never really worked out for me."

"And your father?"

"He was out of the picture the second my mother was pregnant."

He shook his head slightly. "Coward. Both of them."

"I don't judge them. They made the right decision."

He raised an eyebrow.

"I wouldn't want to be raised by parents that didn't want me. It's not a healthy environment. I'm sure I was better off in the system. I had what I needed, and I turned out fine. Of course, I wish I had a family like most people, but it's okay that I didn't. Nothing to be sad about."

He chuckled quietly, shaking his head at the same time.

"What's that supposed to mean?"

"You continue to surprise me."

I knew he wouldn't laugh at me over something like that, so there had to be a different meaning behind his words. "In what way?"

"You've been through so much, but you refuse to accept pity. You don't want anyone to feel bad for you. You don't feel bad for yourself. You had a rough start in life, then you married someone who lied to you, but you're still his friend. I laugh at you because it's ridiculous how forgiving you are. It's incredible how self-assured you are. It's hot..."

All my self-doubt disappeared when I heard those words. "Hot?"

"Very." He pulled me into him and kissed me on the neck. "I hate the damsel-in-distress type. I like a strong woman, a woman who handles her own shit with grace."

"When did you realize what kind of woman you liked? I thought you weren't picky?"

His blue eyes looked into mine with that hard expression he pulled off so well. "I've never been picky. When it comes to fucking, my standards aren't high. But when it comes to actually being with a woman, I know exactly what I like. And I realized that when I met you." He rolled toward me, keeping my leg hooked over his hip as he moved on top of me. His muscled arms bulged with strength, and he stared down at me.

I was falling for this man—so damn hard.

My hands ran up his chest, and I opened my legs for him, beckoning him to take me. It didn't matter how late it was. It didn't matter if this would have a horrifying end. In that moment, I was so addicted, so obsessed, that nothing could take me away from him.

He slid inside me and made me gasp for breath, his hand moving into my hair at the same time.

My nails sank into his back, and my ankles locked together behind him, anchoring him to me like he might slip away.

He rocked into me as he looked at me, as he enjoyed the combustive chemistry between us. He stared at my lips then my eyes, like he couldn't understand what he enjoyed more.

My lips found his, and I got lost deeper into him, feeling the tide drag me away until I was adrift in the ocean, drowning in ecstasy. My heels dug into his back, and I moaned in his mouth, letting this man have all of me while I took all of him. When I got lost in Finn, there was nothing outside these four walls. We were isolated from the rest of the world, free to enjoy each other in secret. This would end eventually, and more than likely, it would end badly. But that didn't matter. It wasn't today's problem.

It was tomorrow's problem.

18

COLTON

Pepper had a large shipment come in Saturday afternoon, so Stella and I stopped by to help her organize everything. There were boxes of panties and sexy thongs and lots of various pieces of lingerie, things with ridiculous price tags. I hung up a bodysuit on the hanger then hooked it on the metal stand. "Like that?"

"Are you serious? Would you buy that?" Stella adjusted the material on the hanger, straightened it out, and then put it farther back. "Smaller sizes go first. Bigger sizes in the back. Come on, Colton."

"It's not like I've ever done this before."

"But you're gay," she countered. "This should be intuition."

I rolled my eyes. "So, I heard through the grapevine you like my boy Zach."

She was in her workout clothes, tight spandex, a workout bra, and a loose-fitting shirt that didn't hide her perfect physique. As a trainer, she worked out every single day with her clients, so she burned calories around the clock. "Maybe."

"Don't play coy with me. We're friends."

"And you're also friends with Zach."

"So?"

"You'll blab to him like the hen that you are."

"What's your point?"

She shook her head. "I do like Zach. But I don't know where it's going. Maybe we'll just have a few dates, and it'll fizzle out. Or maybe it'll go somewhere. I really don't know. I've never had a long-term relationship, so the statistics are working against me."

"Why not?" I asked.

She shrugged. "Haven't found a guy I'm willing to settle down for. I like being single and meeting new people. I'd have to meet someone pretty special to get me to be a one-man kinda woman."

Zach wouldn't want to hear that. The odds were against him.

Pepper came from the back room. "I've got two more boxes of those. They are my best seller, so we'll have two stands of them."

"Hey, Pepper," Stella said. "I have someone I want you to meet. He's in one of my weight-lifting classes. This guy is super-ripped. I mean, I'm not even sure why he's in my class. Maybe he's trying to meet someone. Anyway, I think the two of you should meet."

Instead of looking enthused by the opportunity, she looked affronted. "Uh...I don't know about that."

"Why not?" Stella pressed. "We'll get a beer, and the two of you could talk. This guy is drop-dead gorgeous."

"I'm not a fan of blind dates." Pepper grabbed the bodysuits from the box and started to hang them up. "And if he's so hot, why won't you go out with him?"

"I flirted with him a few times, but he didn't seem interested. I haven't been on my game lately." Her eyes became downturned as she remembered her rejection by Finn.

"He must be gay," I blurted out. "A guy not interested in his hot trainer? That's odd."

"Does that mean Finn is gay?" Pepper countered.

"Well, no," I admitted. "I still don't know what happened with Finn."

"Anyway..." Stella seemed eager to change the subject. "Let me set something up. I think you'll like this guy."

"What makes you think he'd even want to go out with me?" Pepper asked. "If he's not interested in you, then he won't be interested in me."

"He's new to the area and looking to meet new people," Stella said. "I think you guys would hit it off."

"Uh...I don't think so." Pepper picked up the box and carried it to the counter.

"Why not?" Stella demanded, following her. "It's just a drink. We'll be there too."

"I'm just not looking to date right now." She closed the box and labeled the side with a black permanent marker.

"Because...?" Stella crossed her arms over her chest. "Give me one good reason. It can't be because of Jax. You guys broke up months ago, and it didn't seem like you even liked him that much."

"I just don't want to waste my time." She turned back around, visibly flustered. "When I meet someone I like, I'll go for it. But I want it to be organic. I don't want to be set up with some guy just because he's hot."

"Isn't that the only prerequisite that matters?" Stella asked seriously.

"No," Pepper said with a chuckle. "I appreciate it, but I'll pass." She walked to the back to pick up another box.

She turned to me. "Well, this is happening anyway."

"Don't you think that will piss her off?" I asked.

She shrugged. "Real friends get their friends laid. That's all I know."

∾

When I walked in the door, Soldier sprinted toward me and barked in greeting.

"Hey, man." I leaned down and gave him a good rub on the head, seeing his tongue flop out as he greeted me with excitement. "You're a lot more welcoming than Finn is. He doesn't even say hi to me most of the time."

Soldier barked.

I walked into the living room and found Finn sitting on the couch, clean from a shower. He'd worked the morning shift that day, so he got home at about the same time I did. In sweatpants and without a shirt, he looked like he was ready to stay in for the evening. "Your dog is a lot nicer than you are."

"Good. He makes up for my rudeness."

I grabbed a beer from the fridge then sat down.

Soldier moved to the couch beside Finn and sat down, turning into a loyal companion right away.

Finn rubbed his head without looking at him.

"We are going out tonight if you want to join us."

Finn's eyes were glued to the TV, watching the news as it detailed the war happening in the Middle East. He didn't seem to hear a word I said.

"You okay, man?"

Finn grabbed the remote and changed the channel. Once something else was on, he changed his mood. "Who's we?"

"All of us. We're heading to the bar. Tom is coming. It's about time you pick up a woman."

"Don't worry about my sex life, Colton. I never ask you about yours."

"Because you know I have one," I teased. "Isn't that crazy? I'm the stud, and you're the one sleeping alone."

He slowly turned toward me, the fire in his eyes. "When are you moving out?"

I chuckled. "In a few more weeks. Just need to get another paycheck."

"If I give you the money, will you leave now?" he asked, dead serious.

"You know I don't take charity."

"It's not charity," he said. "It's a threat."

I looked away from my brother, knowing it was easy to ignite his sarcastic wrath. "I thought having a dog would make this place dirty and covered in hair, but it's super clean. Whoever said pets were dirty was full of it."

Finn turned back to the TV, one arm hanging over the back of the couch. "Because I clean it, idiot."

"Every day?" I asked incredulously.

He nodded. "I can't stand a dirty home."

"I guess that makes more sense. So, you want to come with us or not?"

"Sure. But are you just inviting me so you have a ride?"

"Psh, no. I've got a man for that now. When we met, the first thing I asked him was if he had a car."

Finn turned to me, his eyebrow raised. "I really hope not."

"Come on, I'm kidding. You know the first thing I asked was if he had a big package."

Finn rose to his feet and, his dog followed him. "I'll get dressed and meet you there."

"Wait, you aren't going to give me a ride?"

"Nope," he said as he walked away. "Have your big-dick boyfriend pick you up."

19

PEPPER

I was just about to step out of my apartment when my phone vibrated with a text message from Finn. *Choose your outfit wisely. If you look anything like you did last time, I'll fuck you in the men's bathroom.* I stared at the message as the bumps formed up and down my arms. This man could pull off comments like that and make them so sexy. Even when they were controlling, possessive, and a little threatening, he still made it work.

That's romantic.

Romance is overrated. Fucking is not.

I stepped out of my apartment and locked the door.

"Hey, Pepper."

I turned around to see Damon, who was dressed in a hoodie and sweatpants. "No big plans tonight?"

"What gave me away?" he said with a chuckle. "I'm

glad I ran into you, actually. I'm moving out of the apartment."

"What? You are?" He'd just moved in a few months ago. He was already leaving? "Why?"

"I've decided I need a new start. My ex and I have the same mutual friends, and it seems like I can't escape her. I got a job offer in California, so I'm relocating. I'm not a big fan of perpetual rain, so it works for me."

"Wow..." That was a lot of information to process in the hallway. "Well...I'm happy for you."

"Thanks. I'll be gone by the end of the week."

That meant the apartment would be available again, and Colton could move back in. But if he lived across the hall from me, it would be impossible to sneak around with Finn. Colton would wonder where I went every weekend and most weekday nights. He would basically have full surveillance on the place. But if I didn't mention the apartment was available, and someone else moved in, he would wonder why I didn't tell him...and that would start a series of questions. "I wish you the best of luck."

"Thanks. And good luck to you too." He gave me a hug before he entered his apartment.

I left my building and took a cab to the bar. I wore a black dress with matching pumps. It had a deep neckline, the kind that forced me to tape my nipples. I hadn't known Finn was going to join us, and now that I did, I was grateful for my choice of outfit.

It would drive him crazy.

I walked inside and found Colton, Zach, and Tatum sitting in a booth.

Tatum whistled as I approached their table. "Damn, you are really rocking that dress."

I did a turn in front of the table, like a model on the runway. "The dress is rocking me, actually."

Zach shook his head then looked at Colton. "Dude, I can't believe you're gay after being married to that."

"Actually, that's how I *knew* I was gay," Colton said. "Being married to a perfect ten but still missing something...it was pretty obvious."

As time passed, I got more used to the fact that Colton was just my friend and not my former lover. Now I started to see him as my gay best friend, not the man I'd loved and lost. There seemed to be more closure to our relationship than ever before. If he'd made a comment like that months ago, I probably would have excused myself to the bathroom for a good cry. But now...it didn't bother me at all.

That was because of Finn. He made me feel like the most desirable woman on the planet, someone who had a lot to offer. He chased away all my fears and self-doubt. He invigorated me with new strength. "I'm gonna get a drink. Anyone want anything?"

"Ooh...I'll take another beer." Colton held up his empty bottle.

"Alright." I walked to the bar, grabbed a couple of drinks, and then returned to the booth. We would have to relocate to a standing table when everyone else arrived because there wasn't enough room for all of us. I was excited for Finn to walk through the door, sexy in his sleeves of ink and hard body, but I dreaded watching every straight woman buy him a drink.

"Stella just walked in," Zach said, his eyes narrowing. "But she's with some other guy...a hot guy."

"A hot guy?" Colton turned around. "Where?"

I saw Stella head to our table in a sparkly dress with heels, her legs so toned, they looked strong as hell. Next to her was a handsome guy with ripped arms and a nice smile. I thought it was strange Stella would bring some other guy to the bar when Zach was there. But then I realized who he was.

Oh shit.

"Hey, guys." Stella patted her hand on her friend's arm. "I want you guys to meet Tyson. He's in one of my classes." Then she turned to me. "Pepper, this is the guy I was telling you about."

Shit. Shit. Shit. "Uh...nice to meet you."

He smiled as his eyes turned affectionate. "Nice to meet you too." He shook my hand, and judging by the appreciative way he looked at my curves, he liked what he saw. It didn't make any sense to me why he preferred me to Stella, the supermodel, but he definitely took the bait.

I shouldn't have worn this dress.

"Let's move to a table," Stella said. "Way too cramped over here."

We grabbed our drinks and made the move, and my heart was racing a million miles a minute. Finn would walk in the door any minute, a temperamental veteran who could kill a man and also save him from the brink of death. He would know I had nothing to do with this, but it would also make the night insufferable. Last time we were together, I'd made it clear that I was his...and only his.

"I'd like to buy you a drink, but it seems like you've got a fresh one. But the next round is on me." He had tanned skin, muscled arms and a powerful chest, and his smile was even more hypnotic. His attitude was innately friendly, not cold and standoffish like Finn's. He headed to the bar and left me alone with my friends.

I immediately rounded on Stella. "What the hell?"

"What the hell, what?" She feigned innocence, as if she weren't doing the exact thing I didn't want her to do. "He's hot."

Colton nodded in agreement. "Super-hot."

Zach even agreed. "I'm into the ladies, but yeah, he's got it going on."

"Doesn't matter how hot he is," I snapped. "I told you I didn't want to be set up."

"Jesus, calm down." She raised her hands then lowered them, like she was bringing down the volume. "Why do you have such a problem with this? It's not like I brought some ugly guy who has ten cats. The guy has a good job, his own apartment, and he's actually got manners. You think I would introduce you to a weirdo?"

"Yeah, what is the big deal?" Colton asked. "Why are you getting so upset?"

"Are you already seeing someone?" Zach asked, figuring out the truth much quicker than the others.

"No," I blurted. "I just...wanted to be by myself for a while."

"That doesn't make any sense," Stella said. "You went from wanting a one-night stand with Jax to swearing off men. What's that about?"

"I haven't sworn off men." I was deeply addicted to one man in particular, a man I couldn't get enough of. Whenever we were together, I wanted more of him. And whenever we were apart, I missed him like crazy. I'd found the man I wanted to spend my nights with... but I could never tell them that. "I just—"

"Then shut up and be charming," Stella said. "You look hot as hell in that dress, so work it, bitch."

"You do look really hot," Tatum said in agreement.

"He didn't hesitate to check you out when he came to the table."

This was officially a nightmare. Finn would arrive, lose his shit, and then he would be talking to a bunch of women at the bar because I wasn't available. I would have to play nice with this guy while Finn drove me crazy.

And tonight was supposed to be fun...

"I'M FROM PORTLAND." Tyson drank a beer while he stood beside me, telling me about his relocation to Seattle.

I was disappointed in his drink choice. He drank beer—not scotch. "And what brings you here?"

"A job opened up here, and I wanted to take it."

"What kind of job?" I pretended to be interested so I wouldn't seem rude, but my eyes kept glancing at the door, fearing the moment when Finn would walk inside.

"I'm a physical therapist. There's this great orthopedics place in town that works with the Seahawks. When they had an opening, I applied. And I'm shocked that I got it. I'll be working with the players during their recovery."

It was an interesting job, but I found it boring.

"Wow, that's cool." It's not like he was a retired veteran who had saved countless lives…like Finn.

At that moment, Finn stepped inside. It was raining outside, so he wore a black leather jacket over his t-shirt. He was already sexy as it was, but paired with a leather jacket, he looked combustive. He glanced around the bar, searching for us and ignoring all the women who immediately focused their gazes on his face. Their lips turned dry, their heart rates picked up, and they imagined their ankles locked around his waist.

Nope, he was mine.

He approached the table, his eyes settling on me. He looked me up and down, silently undressing me and fucking me, and then he looked at the man beside me. His eyes brimmed with a promise of war, of blood-shed and death.

My neck suddenly felt hot with my rapid pulse.

"Cool jacket," Zach said. "I've never seen you wear anything but t-shirts."

Finn didn't even look at him. "Storm is coming." He looked at me again, his eyes drilling into my skin with possessiveness, and then he walked to the bar to get himself a drink.

I finally took a breath when he was gone, feeling safer when there were a few dozen feet between us.

Tyson didn't notice anything. He kept talking. "So,

you own a lingerie shop? I don't mean to sound crass, but that's super-sexy."

"Thanks...I get that a lot."

He kept talking, and then Finn returned with a glass of scotch. He stood beside me, on the other side of Tyson. His arm gently brushed against mine, like he wanted me to know he was there.

Tyson's eyes moved past my frame, noticing the way Finn stood so close to me. "Is this another friend of yours?"

No, definitely not a friend. "This is Finn."

"Nice to meet you." Tyson stuck out his hand to shake Finn's.

Finn didn't return the gesture.

I held my breath as I felt the tension increase, as Finn's rage filled the air around us.

God, this was going to end badly.

Finn finally sucked it up and shook his hand. "You are?"

"Tyson," he answered. "Stella kinda set us up on a date."

I was grateful he said that so Finn would understand the unfortunate position I was in. Tyson wasn't just some random guy who bought me a drink. He was directly connected to the group, so I couldn't just shake him off.

Finn kept staring at him but didn't say anything.

Maybe if Tyson were more intuitive, he would

notice all the subtle alarms in the air. Finn was obviously pissed, but Tyson couldn't pick up on that. He turned back to me. "So tell me more about yourself. I already like everything I've heard."

I wanted to get rid of this guy, but I had no idea clue how to do it without being rude. Maybe if I hadn't been involved with Finn, I might actually like this guy and want it to go somewhere, but since I was already sleeping with a man I adored, I wanted to shake him. An idea popped into my head, and it was so convenient that I was grateful for having a gay ex-husband. "Well, I'm divorced." I imagined Finn was relieved once I preferred that avenue of discussion.

"Ohh..." Tyson nodded slowly. "That must have been rough."

"Yeah, a bit. My husband realized he was gay and left me. Actually, that's him right there." I nodded to Colton, who was talking to Tom, with his arm wrapped around his shoulders.

Tyson glanced at them then turned back to me. "Ohh...that's interesting." He clearly didn't know how to react to that information. It was a lot to take in in a matter of seconds, especially when he could see my ex directly across the table. "Looks like you guys are on good terms."

"Yeah, we are." The tone in our interaction shifted immediately, and it was obvious Tyson didn't dig me anymore. Being divorced at such a young age was a turnoff, and knowing that I was married to a man who ended up being gay wasn't attractive either. The news had the desired effect, and he lost interest.

Mission accomplished.

"WHAT THE HELL WAS THAT?" At the end of the night when Tyson left, Stella turned on me. "Why would you tell him about Colton so nonchalantly?"

Finn had remained at the table with the group, even though free drinks were piling up in front of him. The only drink he ever paid for was the first one he'd ordered. The rest were paid for by male and female admirers. He was in a much better mood once Tyson left.

"Because I didn't tell Jax about him, and it blew up in my face. I want to be with a guy who doesn't have a problem with my past, and if he does, I don't want to waste my time." It was the perfect answer, but it was also the truth. I loved that Finn couldn't care less that I'd been married to a man who decided he was gay. He was never threatened by it and never thought less of me for it.

"That's fine," Stella said. "But did you have to drop that piece of information right when you met him? Let him get to know you before you chase him off."

"If he were a real man, he wouldn't care about her

past," Finn chimed in, even though he hadn't participated in the conversation the entire night. "He wouldn't care about the men who came before him. He wouldn't care about her mistakes and regrets. He would see a beautiful woman looking fine in a dress, and that would be all that mattered. Pepper is right for weeding out the losers. And that guy was definitely a loser."

Stella pouted her lips. "But he was so hot."

"I've seen better." I blurted that out without thinking, picturing Finn's naked body on top of mine.

Finn turned his head slightly in my direction.

"Well, then I'll never set you up again," Stella said. "Friends get their friends laid. I was just trying to do right by you."

"I know. And I appreciate it. But I'm just not ready right now. Whenever I am, we'll revisit it." One day, Finn and I would be over. I had no idea what would happen, but ending up in a white dress simply wasn't possible. He would break my heart eventually...and then I would want to fling myself at the next guy I saw.

"Well, hopefully, I'll be able to find someone hot by then," Stella said. "They're hard to find."

"She's right," Zach said. "We aren't easy to locate in the wild." He turned to Stella and winked.

Now that the nightmare was finally over, I needed another drink. "Excuse me." I returned to the bar, got the bartender's attention, and ordered a vodka cranberry—making it a double.

Finn appeared at my side with his full glass in hand.

"I had no control over what happened."

"I know." His deep voice was calm and suave as usual. "I made it clear your pussy was mine, and you wouldn't disobey me."

I turned to him, slightly offended by the use of the term "disobey" but also aroused by his ownership. I didn't want to be with anyone else, and I was glad he didn't want me to be with anyone else either. I was also touched by his confidence that I would be faithful to him. "I don't see how this can go on much longer. We can't keep up the charade for more than a few months. They'll notice that I never date and you never date. And then my neighbor across the hall is moving out, so Colton will be moving back in soon…"

"Have you told Colton?"

"No. But I can't hide it from him. He'll realize my neighbor is gone eventually and will wonder why I never told him. It'll open up his suspicion, and he'll examine me until he discovers our secret." There was no way we could keep carrying on this affair. It would bite us in the ass in the end.

Finn stayed quiet beside me, his eyes drilling into the side of my face.

The bartender handed me my drink, and I downed

half of it in one go. I didn't want to keep lying to the people in my life. I didn't want to keep lying to Colton either. He told me all the details of his relationship with Tom, and I felt lonely not telling him about Finn. Colton was the person I used to confide everything to. Now that I didn't share my life with him...I felt empty. "I think I'm going to tell him."

Finn downed his scotch until the glass was empty.

"I don't want to keep lying to him. I don't want to keep sneaking around. I just... It's not me."

He stared straight ahead and looked at nothing in particular. Then he leaned forward, putting his arms on the bar as he bowed his head.

I waited for him to tell me we should just end this relationship for good. It was better than coming clean to his brother and being honest about our betrayal. Finn probably didn't want to go down that road, and since he wasn't looking for anything serious, it wouldn't make sense for him to put his relationship with Colton at risk. "I should be the one to talk to him."

Shocked, I stilled at his words. I stared into my drink before I slowly turned toward him, unable to believe the words that just came out of his mouth.

He continued to keep his bed bowed before he sighed and righted himself. "You've done nothing wrong. You're a single woman who doesn't owe him anything. He was the one who lied to you, wasted your time, and broke your heart. I know you've forgiven him and you guys are friends...but he has no right to be upset with you. Me, on the other hand, I'm the one in the wrong. I'm the one who crossed the line. I'm the one who was disloyal. I should be the one to tell him."

I didn't want this to ruin their relationship. They'd just become close again, and I didn't want them to be ripped apart. I wasn't worth it. "Maybe you should wait until he has his own apartment, that way he can have some space."

"Or maybe doing it while he lives with me is better. We'll be forced to be together, so he can forgive me and let it go."

"He'll be upset..."

"I know. But he'll see reason eventually."

I couldn't believe this was happening. We were really going to come clean. "When are you going to do it?"

He leaned against the counter and turned toward me, leaning against the counter so he could face me head on. In that black leather jacket, he looked so delicious, so unbelievably sexy. "When the time is right."

"Are you sure you want to do this?" We'd never talked about having a serious relationship. We didn't talk about marriage and kids. We hadn't even talked about love. Did it make sense to tell Colton about our relationship when we didn't know how we felt? If we thought there was a possibility we might feel that way in the future. There was no question that Finn was different with me, that he was affectionate, soft, and monogamous. But could he offer more than that someday?

He looked me in the eye without blinking, full of the strength he displayed on a daily basis. "Yes."

20

COLTON

The Uber stopped in front of the house, and I hopped out of the car and walked to the front door. It was Sunday morning and I'd had a great night with Tom last night, but he had plans today and kicked me out.

I let myself inside and was greeted by Soldier's wagging tail and his eager paws. He stood on his hind legs and greeted me with a quiet bark.

"Hey, boy." I scratched him by the ears then lowered him to the floor. Soldier was still a brand-new addition to our lives, but I'd become so comfortable with him. Now I was used to having him around. He was a beautiful and affectionate dog, and I kinda never wanted to move out because I would miss him.

I moved into the kitchen and found Finn sitting at

the table, reading the paper with a mug of hot coffee in front of him.

"Morning." I poured myself a glass then took the seat across from him.

"Morning." He folded his paper and set it on the surface of the table. There was a bottle of scotch beside his glass, like he'd been spiking his morning coffee with booze. Instead of ignoring me like he usually did, he looked me straight in the eye.

I sipped my coffee and held his gaze, my eyebrow raised. "What?"

"I didn't say anything."

"But you're looking at me."

"I can't look at you?"

"It's just strange, is all." I blew the steam off my coffee and took a drink.

"Long night?"

"No, it was a short night. Time flies when you're having fun, right?" I winked.

Instead of smiling at my joke, he still seemed tense, as if there was something on his mind, but he refused to share it with me. He leaned forward over the table and rested his arms on the surface.

"Go home with anyone last night?"

"No."

My brother made absolutely no sense. One minute, he was getting more pussy than any other guy in the world without paying for it. But now he was so celibate, he seemed like a monk. It was strange, to say the least. "Too bad it didn't work out between Pepper and Tyson. That guy was hot." I wanted Pepper to end up with a perfect guy, a man who could erase all of my mistakes. They would have beautiful children, and I would be an uncle to those adorable babies.

His eyes narrowed slightly.

My brother was always moody and formidable, but he seemed particularly sour this early in the morning. "Something on your mind?"

"Yes."

"Alright..." I took a drink of my coffee. "You want to talk about it?" My brother never discussed his feelings, so I doubted he wanted to bare his soul to me over coffee.

He glanced at his coffee before he looked me in the eye again. "There's something I want to talk to you about."

That was never a good sign. "Okay..."

He took another drink of his coffee, licked his lips, and then released a quiet sigh. "I know this will be hard for you to hear, but keep an open mind."

"I'm liking this less and less..."

He held my gaze for a long time, gathering his thoughts before he finally dropped his news. "I've had a thing for Pepper since the moment I met her. I did my best to ignore it and forget about her, but it's become impossible. I want to ask her out...if you're cool with it."

My eyes focused on his face with powerful intensity, and my chest turned rigid because I stopped breathing. He was talking about Pepper, my ex-wife, the woman I had a relationship with for five years. My brother, my flesh and blood, just asked if he could be with her. That crossed so many lines that it was hard to process what he just said. "Cool with it...?" Both of my eyebrows furrowed because the request was ridiculous. "You want to know if I would be cool with you asking out my wife?"

"*Ex*-wife."

"Whatever." I slammed my hand down. "I shouldn't even have to explain why that's inappropriate. Friends and family don't date your ex, let alone your ex-wife. That's wrong on so many levels, Finn."

He held my gaze without a hint of remorse. "You left her because you realized you were gay."

"What does that matter?" I snapped. "What if I'd left her for another woman? Would that make it okay for you to go after her? No, it doesn't make a difference. You're acting like my being gay gives you permission when it shouldn't make a difference at all."

He pressed his lips tightly together.

"Finn, there are so many women in Seattle, so many gorgeous women, and you can have anyone you want. You seriously pick the one woman who's off-limits? The one I was married to? The one who is my best friend? That's so stupid, it hurts my brain." I threw my arms in the air. "No, I'm not cool with it. I shouldn't have to be cool with it. She still has my last name."

He stared at me without blinking, his fingers resting around his mug.

I felt the ferocity in my chest, the betrayal in my blood. "I can't believe you would even ask me that."

"You're seeing someone, and you don't care if she's dating."

"That's totally different, and you know it."

"You said you want her to end up with a good guy. I'm a doctor and a veteran—"

"Who said you were a good guy?" Maybe I should calm down before we continued this conversation, but now I was caught up in the heat of the moment. "You're the biggest player I know. You even told me you never want to get married or have kids. You only want Pepper so you can use her for a few weeks and dump her. No, you aren't a good guy, Finn."

His eyes fell slightly, as if he was actually offended by what I said.

"She wants a husband and a family. She wants a man who's going to stick around. You think I'd let a womanizer like you go anywhere near her?" I asked incredulously. "Fuck no."

"I'm not a womanizer."

"Oh?" I mocked. "Then what are you? How many relationships have you been in?"

His eyes narrowed. "Just because I haven't been in a relationship doesn't mean I'm a womanizer. I'm up front about my intentions. I don't pretend I'm going to call and never do. Women know exactly what they are getting from me."

"Which is?" I challenged.

Finn sighed quietly when he realized he'd backed himself into a corner.

"She's already been hurt enough. I'm not going to let you fuck her over when she's still vulnerable."

"She's stronger than you give her credit for."

"She's the strongest person I know," I argued. "But she has her limits. I won't let you be the one who breaks them."

Finn relaxed against the wooden chair and moved his arms to the armrests. He stared at me as the silence passed, as he considered his next argument.

It didn't matter what argument he gave, my answer would stay the same. "The answer is no, Finn. I won't change my mind. And I'm pretty fucking ticked that you would even ask."

He gripped the wood underneath his fingers until his knuckles turned white. "Pepper has done a lot for you, Colt. She stayed loyal to you even after you told her your marriage was a lie. She's still friends with you to this day. And she even..." He shut his mouth and released the wood under his grip.

"She what?"

His nostrils flared slightly before he controlled his rage. "There's nothing she wouldn't do for you. You're being an asshole for not doing the same for her."

"I'm an asshole because I don't want my brother to fuck my wife?"

"*Ex*-wife," he hissed. "Let's not forget that you were too much of a coward to come clean about who you really were. You wasted five years of her life when you always knew she wasn't the right one. You hurt her self-esteem and her pride. You don't get to pull that shit and then say I'm not good enough for her."

"You aren't good enough for her."

He jerked slightly, like that insult wounded him.

I shook my head. "This is unbelievable. I thought I saw something between you, but I kept telling myself my brother would never do that. He's too honorable."

"And don't you think the fact that I'm asking you indicates how I feel about her? That I'm willing to risk my relationship with you to be with her? Do you really think we would be having this conversation if she didn't mean something to me?"

"You just want her because you can't have her."

He looked away, like he was stopping himself from saying something he would regret. "That's not it, Colt."

"It is it. Because you can't have her—end of story." I

pushed back my chair and rose to my feet. "I see the end better than the beginning. You would use her for a few weeks, get her to fall for you like all the other women, and then dump her. You'd crush her. You'd never offer her anything she deserves. I won't stand by and let that happen. She's still my family. She's more of my family than you've ever been."

He clenched his jaw as if he wanted to explode like a volcano. "I didn't realize you thought so little of me."

"I didn't." I looked down at him, furious. "But I do now." I walked away and headed to the front door, prepared to get an Uber and get the hell out of there.

Finn's footsteps followed me. "Colt."

"Fuck off." I got to the front door.

Finn pushed it shut then blocked the way. "Give me a chance to see where it goes. You assume I'm going to hurt her, but I wouldn't go to all these lengths if I didn't really feel something for her."

"Have you changed your thoughts on marriage and kids?"

He was quiet.

"Because if you aren't open to that, then this is doomed to fail. And if there's no chance of success, I won't let you use her heart for target practice. Go fuck someone else, Finn. Pepper is mine. She's the one person in my life who has preferred me over you. Mom and Dad consider you their favorite because you're the war hero. Girls in school always said you were the hot one. Well, Pepper and I have something special even if we aren't in love anymore. I'm not going to let you destroy that."

"I would never interfere with your friendship, Colton. I don't care if you love each other. I don't care if you sleep in her bed with her after a bad day. My relationship with her has nothing to do with yours."

"But what happens when you dump her?"

"What if she dumps me?" he countered. "You assume I'm the heartbreaker, but she's smart, gorgeous, and perfect. Maybe she'll break my heart. Did you ever think of that?"

I rolled my eyes. "That's not how this is going to go, and we both know it. No matter how it ends, it'll affect my relationship with her. You two won't be able to be in the same room together, she won't be able to come over for the holidays because you'll be there, and then I won't be able to be in the same room with both of you at the same time. That affects me, Finn."

"Then I'll step back," he said. "It's not like you like me very much anyway, right?" He stepped back, his rugged face hard with stoicism. If he was hurt, he hid it under his brooding masculinity.

"I never said that."

"You said it a lot during this conversation. I'm not good enough for Pepper. I'm not a good guy. I don't deserve her. I'm just some asshole who's going to break her heart. That's what you said, right?"

I didn't know what to say, how to erase the words I'd spoken.

"So I'll step back. I'll spend the holidays alone so you can keep Pepper in your life...since she's more important to you." He stepped back and turned away.

"That's not what I want, Finn. I need both of you in my life—not just one of you."

He stopped walking, his back still turned to me.

I knew I'd wounded my brother with all the horrible things I'd just said, but I didn't know how to take them back. I didn't know if I even should. I meant every word because I was protective of Pepper.

He slowly turned around and faced me again. "Fine. I won't ask her out."

I was relieved I finally got him to back off. "Good."

He kept staring at me like he had more to say. "But if you really love Pepper, you would step aside and let her have whatever she wants, whatever makes her happy. If I asked her out and she said yes, then you should step aside. Maybe I'm the man who could make her happy, but we'll never know. Love isn't selfish, Colton. Real love is selfless. And Pepper has been nothing but selfless when it comes to you... You should be the same for her."

21

COLTON

I drank my beer at the bar and swallowed my feelings.

"Wow...Finn wants Pepper." Zach sat across from me and shook his head.

I still couldn't believe it either. I looked down at the table as I reflected on our conversation, on the bomb he'd dropped on my head. "I can't believe he asked me. That would be like you asking me if you could date Pepper."

"Yeah, you wouldn't be happy about that."

"I'm right for being upset, right?" I looked up at him, needing validation.

"Yeah, completely. She's not just some woman you've been with in the past... She's your ex-wife. I think anyone with a brain could figure out how wrong that is."

"Could you imagine them dating?" I asked incredulously. "Coming to holidays at my family's place together? Wouldn't that be weird?"

He shrugged. "I never thought about it that way..."

"He said I was selfish for saying no."

"I don't know... It is weird. You were married to her for years."

"He said it shouldn't matter since I'm gay. But I don't see why that makes a difference. What if I married another woman and had two kids with her? Would that make it okay for him to date my ex-wife? No."

"Yeah," he said in agreement. "That would be awkward as hell."

"It's no different. I just don't understand why Finn has to want Pepper when there are so many women in this city."

"In his defense, Pepper is pretty cool. She's pretty, funny, smart, successful...the list goes on." He drank his beer as his eyes turned glossy. "On that account, I can't blame him. But yeah, it's his younger brother's ex-wife...sounds like a Greek tragedy."

I knew I was right for being upset, but I couldn't help but feel guilty. "He said he would drop it."

"Then your problem is solved."

"But I think I hurt his feelings a bit..."

"And he hurt yours."

"But I said things about his character. I meant them

at the time, but I didn't realize how harsh they sounded until I saw his face. I feel bad about it..."

"The conversation wouldn't have happened if he hadn't tried to hook up with Pepper."

"Yeah...I was just angry."

"So...are you going to tell Pepper?"

If Finn was asking if he could date her, then I would assume she had no idea. If I told her, it would make things awkward every time they were in a room together. It was probably best to keep it a secret. "No. I don't think she has any idea."

"Then you can forget this whole thing happened."

"Yeah..." I was still pretty shaken up about it, but maybe in time, I would let it go. My feelings were so complicated. I was angry Finn had crossed the line, but I also felt guilty for not giving him what he wanted. I felt like the bad guy, when I had every right to feel the way I did. Finn understood that, right?

Or did he want her so much that he didn't care?

I CAME HOME LATE that evening and found him sitting on the couch with Soldier. I'd drunk most of the evening with Zach, trying to clear my thoughts and dissipate my anger. I still lived with my brother, so I couldn't be angry with him forever.

He tore his gaze away from the TV and glanced at me, but he didn't say anything.

I stood behind the couch and tried to think of something to say. Both of us were upset with each other, and it was a shame because our relationship had grown so much since he'd returned from the military. "Look, I know I said some mean things back there... I do think you're a good guy. I just don't think you're right for Pepper, that's all."

He kept looking at the TV.

"I don't want this to ruin our relationship. That's one of the reasons I don't want you to date her in the first place. Look at the damage it's already caused. This is why you don't date each other's exes."

"The damage resulted because of your reaction to it." He turned to me. "I calmly asked if it would be okay, but you blew up at me."

"Because I was shocked you asked in the first place."

He grabbed the remote and turned off the TV. "I asked because that's how much I want her, that's how much she means to me. I feel something with her that I've never felt with anyone else. Yes, I have a reputation as a player, but I would never treat Pepper like that. She's different. I would never get involved with her unless it was different."

"Are you in love with her?" I asked bluntly. If he was, then that would be a different story. It would still be wrong, but at least it would be a situation we couldn't ignore. I would have to step aside and let it happen. Love was strong...love had a future. Anything less than that was too risky.

"How can I answer that if I haven't had a chance to be with her?" He rested his arms on his knees as he stared at me.

"Then how do you know it's different?"

"Because I want to be with her, not just sleep with her. I want to take her out jogging with Soldier and me—"

"Pepper doesn't jog."

"A walk, then," he snapped. "I want more than sex. I want a relationship. I don't know where that relationship will go. Maybe it will die out in a few weeks or months. I have no idea. I can't promise you I'll marry her. But I know that this isn't some hit-it-and-quit-it kind of stunt. I actually respect her." He gave me another speech to change my mind, to show how serious he was about this.

But I couldn't change the way I felt. It made me uncomfortable, angry, and I knew it would end badly. It was in my best interest, as well as Pepper's. Finn would find new tail to chase next week. This would all just be a bad memory. "The answer is no, Finn. Sorry."

His eyes fell in disappointment before he bowed his head. He didn't make another argument. He was quiet in his defeat, finally giving up. "If she knew about this, she would be disappointed in you."

"No, she wouldn't. Let's not forget that I know her better than you ever will."

PEPPER and I met for lunch at Mega Shake.

I tried to be strong and order the salad with light dressing, but I caved and got the burger and fries. But I didn't get the shake, so that was something to be proud of.

Pepper ate whatever she wanted because she could pull it off. She popped the fries into her mouth then looked at me as she drank her root beer. "Something wrong? You're awfully quiet."

"It's just been a long week..."

"Something happen with Tom?" She could read my mood well, so I would have to come up with a story. Otherwise, she would keep pestering me.

"No. I had a fight with Finn..."

"Oh..." She was about to grab more fries, but she pulled her hand away and stopped eating. "What did you fight about?" Her tone dropped as her eyes moved down to her food.

"Just stupid stuff...dishes, chores, hogging the laundry machine. Stuff like that."

She looked up again, her eyes less timid. Her hand

reached for the fries, and she placed a few inside her mouth. "That's bound to happen."

"And he's nicer to Soldier than he is to me."

"Well, Soldier is a lot cuter."

I rolled my eyes. "I think I need to get my own place soon. The house is big, but not big enough for the two of us."

"Well, Damon just moved out."

"The cutie across the hall?" I asked in surprise.

"Yep. Moved to California."

"That sucks."

She shrugged. "Nothing was going to happen anyway."

"Because you aren't ready to date?"

"Yeah..."

"Tyson was super-cute, but you blew him off. Guess you really aren't ready."

"Yeah...I'll know when it's right."

Then telling Finn to back off was definitely the best decision. She didn't want anything romantic right now, let alone a complicated offer from my brother. That would be more drama for her. Then she would have to deal with the uncomfortable task of telling him no... and making it awkward. "I'm sure you will. So, that apartment is available again?"

"I think so."

"Wow, that's perfect. I miss that place. And we can be right next door to each other again."

"Yeah, like old times."

I was thrilled to leave Finn's house and be close to Pepper again. I missed seeing her every morning. I missed watching her walk into my apartment and hijack my food. I missed our closeness. No matter how successful my relationship with Tom was, it would never compare to the special thing I had with Pepper. I needed it in my life to be happy. "Awesome. I'll talk to the manager after work today. Finn will be happy to get his space back, and I'll be happy to let you steal all my food again."

"I don't steal *all* your food," she countered.

"Just breakfast every morning," I teased. "And a lifetime supply of coffee."

"Well, you got the coffeemaker in the divorce."

"It's like twenty-five bucks. Don't be so cheap."

She threw a fry at my nose. "I paid for your lunch. Now look who's cheap."

It bounced off my face and landed in my tray. I picked it up and ate it, chuckling at her comeback. The easiness of this relationship was what I loved about it. It was the most stable relationship I'd ever been in. I felt more love from her than I ever did my own parents. How could I risk the best thing in my life by giving Finn my permission? Pepper would get hurt. I would get hurt. There was too much at risk.

I couldn't risk the best thing that ever happened to me.

22

PEPPER

I t was late in the evening when a knock sounded on the door. I was sitting on the couch with a glass of wine, with paperwork on the coffee table. The nice thing about owning my own business was I got to be the boss. But that also meant I had to take work home after hours. Even when I wasn't on the clock, I thought about the success of my business.

I assumed it was Finn because no one else would stop by unannounced.

My heart started to thump.

I opened the door and found him on the other side, looking irresistible in his t-shirt and jeans. A shadow was on his jaw because he'd skipped the shave that morning. It was unusual for him to forgo his hygiene process, but the stubble looked good on him. His eyes bored into mine with their usual intensity, but there was definitely a hint of something else, something darker. Being with Finn these last few months had taught me how to read him. To a stranger, he looked moody all the time, but for me, I could see the difference. "Something wrong?"

He stared at me for several heartbeats before he welcomed himself inside my apartment. He shut the door behind him then slid his hand up my neck and deep into my hair. His kiss accompanied the movement, his soft lips taking mine with masculine ownership. His arm circled my waist and squeezed me against his hard body.

I stopped worrying about his troubles and only cared about his desire. My one hand gripped his arm while the other snaked up his chest. The breath left my lungs as he took all of it, devouring me like his favorite meal.

He breathed into my mouth as he kissed me, his body guiding me backward toward the bedroom. When we reached the foot of the bed, he squeezed me against his chest then lifted me onto the bed.

I was in my plaid pajama bottoms and a thin white t-shirt that showed my nipples through the hard fabric. My nipples hardened to diamonds as he yanked my bottoms off then slid my panties down my legs.

I pulled my shirt over my head and watched him stare at my naked body, not the least bit turned off by my lack of makeup. My tits firmed slightly against my body, feeling the cold draft mix with the heat of his gaze. My heartbeat was so strong in my chest, I felt it pound like a drum. My heart matching the cadence of my pulse in my wrists, my body was in hyperdrive. I'd been with this man so many times, but he always made it feel like the first time, the first night we gave in to our passion.

Like a private stripper, he pulled his shirt over his head and revealed the chiseled torso along with his life story written in ink. The dark color of the images didn't mask all the subtle details of his sculpted physique, of all the hard work he put into perfecting his body. He wasn't just visually appealing, but so strong, he was ready for war at any moment. His jeans and boxers came off next, showing the bottom half of his perfect body.

Instead of staring at his best feature, I moved my eyes to his gaze, seeing far more beauty deep inside that gruff soul. My thighs squeezed together because this man was so beautiful on the surface, but I adored everything underneath much more. He was honest, humble, and brave. He had his own insecurities, but I saw a man who'd earned my respect a million times over. I didn't just love his looks, but the appearance of his soul underneath that hard chest. Most women just wanted to sleep with him, and I was no different. But I also felt a lot more for this man.

I felt a lot more for him than anyone else.

Even Colton.

It was a scary thought, to have such strong feelings for a man who wasn't my husband. I'd loved Colton very much, but it was never like this. It was never this intense, this climactic. There was never a threshold of emotion so profound it made my hands shake. The connection I had with Finn was deeper. It was hard to believe the men were brothers because they were so different.

Completely different souls.

Finn moved on top of me and lowered me to the bed, his lips caressing mine as he took control over the situation. His thick arms widened my legs, and he slid inside me, making all of the movements with perfect fluidity.

I gripped his arms and moaned, unprepared for the sensation between my legs. I'd been with this man so many times, but it always caught me off guard how good he felt inside me. My head rolled back, and I felt his lips caress my neck, gliding over the thick vein that led to my jaw and then down to my collarbone.

I moaned and writhed underneath him, throbbing in sexual catharsis. My fingers gripped him while he rocked into me, sliding through my tight arousal where he belonged. My mouth moved to his, and I kissed him as he took me, as he claimed my mind, body, and soul.

This man made me feel confident, made me feel

beautiful. I used to be ashamed of my divorce, but he showed me that a real man wouldn't think less of me, that there was nothing to think less of. He put me back together when no one else did. He made me realize my value, that I was just as desirable as I was before my husband admitted he was gay and left me.

He fixed me when I didn't realize I was broken.

That gratitude mixed with affection and became something much greater. Sleeping with him was wrong, but since it felt so right, I stopped feeling guilty about it. I didn't know where this would go, but I wanted to enjoy the ride as long as possible.

My ALARM WOKE me early the next morning.

Finn was gone.

I got out of bed and walked into the living room, finding him sitting on the couch fully clothed. The TV was off, and he stared at his joined hands between his knees. He didn't look up at me and call me baby. It seemed like he didn't want to look at me at all.

I'd forgotten his demeanor last night because we got swept away by the unbridled passion. The kisses silenced my words, and the deep connection between us chased off everything else.

But now the problem had returned.

I sat beside him on the couch. "What is it?" I knew

it wasn't a problem with us because he made love to me like I was the only woman in the world who mattered. He made me feel like the only woman he'd ever been with.

He still didn't answer.

"Colton told me you had a fight. I'm sure it'll blow over." My hand moved to his.

He slowly turned his face toward me. "He told you that?"

I nodded. "Said living together had become tense. You're fighting about the dishes and the laundry...said he should probably move out and give you your space."

He faced forward again, his hand not reciprocating my affection. He kept it in place, but his fingers showed no signs of life. "That's not it."

"Then what is it?" I whispered. "You've changed your mind about telling him about us?" Maybe now that they were butting heads, he wanted to let things cool down before he dropped this bomb on him. The timing wasn't right.

He was quiet again, still and so silent, it seemed like he was ignoring me. He pulled his hand away and brought them together on his thighs. Eye contact was usually his signature quality. He was never afraid to stare at me to the point I was uncomfortable. But now, that intimacy was gone. He preferred the blank TV instead of my face. "Yes."

I didn't reach for his hand again even though I was desperate. My fingers yearned for his touch, just for the assurance that everything would be alright. He was so distant from me. Last night, we were so entangled, we were practically one person. "Oh..."

He rubbed the back of his neck, like he was a massaging a kink. "I've been thinking about us lately, and I started to wonder if we were making the right decision. Telling Colton will obviously make him upset. It'll cause tension among all three of us."

"But I can't keep lying, Finn."

"I know. Neither can I." His masculine voice deepened slightly. "But I don't think it makes sense to go that route unless this is going somewhere. I like you a lot, Pepper, but you know what I want in life. I'm not looking for a wife. I don't want a family."

The statement felt like a knife right in my throat. "I'm not asking for marriage, Finn. I'm not asking for anything right now... We haven't even had a real relationship."

"I know." He bowed his head slightly. "I just don't think it's worth taking the risk with Colton unless that's what we're fighting for. I don't see anything serious happening between us, so we're putting our relationships with him in jeopardy for nothing."

When I finally understood what was happening, my throat went dry.

Finn was dumping me.

He didn't want me longer than a few weeks. He said I was different from the others, but I wasn't different enough. Our relationship wasn't worth fighting for because we didn't have a relationship at all.

Geez, that hurt.

I knew I shouldn't have expected anything from him because he never really offered anything. He'd never promised me we would have anything. He'd never talked about the future, and he'd never told me he loved me.

I was hurt because I'd fallen for him.

So fucking hard.

In the back of my mind, I guess I'd hoped something more would happen. I'd hoped Finn and I would have a slow relationship that would eventually blossom into forever. He said the sweetest things to me, that I was the kind of woman he wanted.

Maybe my heart absorbed those words too deeply.

Maybe I believed them too much.

Maybe I should have kept my walls up higher instead of letting them crumble.

Maybe I should have remembered that Finn was a player.

Not the boyfriend type.

I did my best to keep my face stoic because I refused to show my pain. He crushed me, but I refused to let him see the debris of my heart. I should have known he was too good to be true. I should have known that this beautiful and perfect man wouldn't seriously want me. Maybe he only wanted me because I was the only woman in the world who was off-limits.

He turned to me after several minutes of silence. "I think it's for the best."

I kept my eyes dry as I nodded slightly. "Yeah... maybe it is."

He kept examining me, like he was looking for signs of my distress.

I refused to show them. I was too stubborn to let that happen.

"I'm sorry." His eyes were full of remorse as he whispered the phrase, like he truly hated what was happening.

Did he hate that we were breaking up? Or did he hate the fact that he hurt me?

I guess it didn't matter.

I cleared my throat so the tears wouldn't be audible in my voice. "Nothing to be sorry for."

He continued to watch me, his eyes not as confident as they usually were. "I hope we can be friends."

The last thing I wanted to do was watch him pick up women at bars and take them home. I didn't want to see all the pretty girls buy him round after round. I didn't want to listen to Colton mention his brother's conquests in passing. That would kill me. But I couldn't cut him out of my life either. That would make things complicated for Colton, which wouldn't be fair. I had to take the high road. "Of course."

He faced forward again and sighed. "I should go." He rose to his feet and headed to the door, dismissing the conversation like he hadn't just broken my heart.

I followed him to the door, using all my strength to keep my composure. Letting my tears fall wouldn't make this easier. Even if he held me, it would just remind me that I had to let him go.

He wasn't mine anymore.

He opened the door then turned around to face me, like he considered kissing me or hugging me goodbye.

But he didn't do either of those things. "I'll see you later." He gave a slight nod then walked away.

Walked away like I meant nothing to him.

I stayed on the threshold and stared at the door across the hall, listening to his footsteps as they grew quieter with distance. He came to my doorstep last night, whisked me away for a night of lovemaking, making me fall head over heels. Then he turned cruel and dropped me the next day.

It was torture.

I shut the door and slowly returned to the couch, moving as if in a trance. I had to get to work and open the store, but work seemed like the least important thing in my life right now. All I could think about was the heat behind my eyes, the tightness of my throat, the storm that was slowly brewing.

The hot tears emerged and streaked down my cheeks.

Then I started to cry.

THE WEEK PASSED IN A BLUR.

My nights were restless, and my days were exhausting.

The most difficult part was pretending to be okay when I wasn't.

I had lunch with Colton, and even though he asked me if something was wrong many times, I lied and said everything was fine. When I went out with Stella and Tatum, I forced a smile on my face and laughed harder than necessary, even when something wasn't that funny. Inside, I was completely dead.

I didn't realize how I felt about Finn until he was gone.

When I'd signed those divorce papers, I was a mess.

But now I was worse.

I wasn't sure what I'd expected out of Finn. It was messy and complicated and there was no future right from the beginning, but that logic didn't cushion my broken heart. I could control my mind, but I couldn't control my feelings.

I didn't see or hear from Finn over the course of the week.

I wasn't sure what I would do once I saw him again.

Could we ever really be friends?

I was sitting on my couch staring at the wall when a knock sounded on the door. "Pepper, it's me."

I recognized Colton's voice and felt foolish for hoping it would be Finn. I opened the door and plastered a fake smile on my face. "What's up?"

He invited himself into the apartment. "I talked to the landlord. I got the apartment back."

"Really?" I asked, doing my best to pretend to be happy. It would be nice having him across the hall again, but I was too numb to feel anything. I started to notice a correlation between Colton and my lovers. Colton seemed to interfere with every romantic relationship I ever had. Maybe I would never have a successful relationship when we were this close. But I still couldn't give him up. "That's awesome. When do you move in?"

"Next week. You can get your free coffee again."

I chuckled. "Yeah...that will be nice."

"So let's go out tonight to celebrate. I'll round everyone up."

The last thing I wanted to do was see Finn, but I couldn't avoid him forever. It was inevitable. Every interaction with him would be painful, until one day, it would just stop hurting. I thought I would never get over my divorce, but I somehow managed that. I could get over this too.

At least, that's what I kept telling myself.

23

COLTON

Finn was in a particularly bad mood that week. He was always short and cold anytime we spoke, and he spent most of his time in his bedroom with the door shut. He didn't watch the game downstairs or cook dinner on the stove. I wasn't even sure what he was eating because he hardly showed his face.

When I came home, he was in the kitchen—by chance. He made a sandwich at the counter with a shadow on his face that was turning into a beard. Things had been tense with us since our last conversation, but it was getting better as time passed. I was angry at him for asking to go after Pepper, but I couldn't be that angry when he asked me first. He didn't go behind my back and do it anyway like a sleazebag. I had to give him credit for that. "I got my old apartment back."

He twisted off the cap of his beer and took a drink. "When do you leave?"

"Next week."

He picked up his sandwich and took a bite.

"Everything alright?" If he was still mad at me about Pepper, he was being dramatic. I was the one who had the right to be angry, but I'd already dropped it. He didn't have an excuse.

"Yeah." He kept eating, ignoring me.

"It seems like you're avoiding me."

"I don't avoid anyone." He set his sandwich down and looked at me.

"You're in your room a lot..."

"I just want to be alone right now. It's my house. I can do whatever the fuck I want." Anger was the undertone to every single word he uttered. His eyes were full of emptiness, and his gaze was full of bitterness.

"I've never seen you not shave before."

"How about you stop worrying about my hygiene and worry about yours?" He only ate half the sandwich before he threw the rest away. He snatched the beer off the counter and began the walk to his bedroom.

I didn't understand Finn's venom, and maybe I never would. "We're going out tonight to celebrate if you want to come."

He stopped in his tracks then turned back to me. "To celebrate what?"

"Getting my old apartment back. You want to come?"

"Why would you even want me to come?" he asked, his eyes narrowed.

"I don't hate you, Finn. You're my brother...you'll always be my brother. I was mad about Pepper in the beginning, but we talked about it and moved on. I'm prepared to drop it if you are."

He drank his beer then looked at the ground.

"We're meeting at eight if you want to join us." I didn't waste any more time on him. I headed to the kitchen to make something to eat. Instead of waiting for scraps, Soldier stayed at Finn's side.

Finn looked at me for another moment before he turned up the stairs.

I watched him go, understanding my brother even less than when he first came to live with me.

"Wow, you look great." I looked Pepper up and down when she walked inside.

"Super-hot," Zach said. "If I didn't have a lady, I would be buying you a drink."

"Thanks," Pepper said. "You guys are sweet."

"We aren't sweet," I argued. "We're being serious."

She smiled then walked to the bar to get a drink.

Finn returned from the bathroom, his jaw clean because he'd shaved before he left the house. He'd styled his hair and put on a shirt that wasn't wrinkly. The second he joined us, he reached for his scotch like it was a crutch.

"You should see how hot Pepper looks when she comes back," Zach said to my brother. "She's wearing this teal dress—"

"Zach." I shut up him just using his name, not wanting to make things awkward with Finn.

Finn wore the same stoic expression, like those words meant nothing to him.

Pepper returned a moment later, her short dress making her green eyes stand out. Her hair was done, and she'd applied her makeup in a slightly different way. She approached the standing table then looked at Finn.

He looked back at her.

She opened her mouth to say something, but nothing came out.

Finn led the conversation. "The guys were just telling me how beautiful you looked. They were right." He took a long drink of his glass until it was empty. "Excuse me, I need another drink." He left the table and headed to the bar.

Pepper watched him go before she turned back to us, her skin noticeably pale. The smile she'd been wearing a moment ago disappeared, and when she looked sad, she wasn't nearly as pretty. She looked down at her vodka cranberry, her mind traveling to a faraway place.

"When are the girls getting here?" I asked Zach.

"Stella had a late class," he explained. "And I think Tatum had a date."

Pepper kept her wide eyes focused on her glass, not even blinking.

"Pepper?"

Her eyes flicked up to mine. "Yeah?"

"Are you alright?" I asked. "You seem...distracted."

She cleared her throat. "Just thinking about work... you know. There's so much stuff I forgot to do at the shop today."

"I'm so glad I don't own a business," Zach said. "Too much work and stress."

"Yeah, it can be hectic," she said quietly.

Zach looked at the bar then nudged me in the side. "Guess who Finn's talking to."

My eyes landed on Layla, the tattooed doctor he worked with in the ER. The beautiful woman stole everyone's attention because she was sexy and exotic, having all those colorful tattoos everywhere. "Yeah, you're right."

Pepper didn't turn around to look.

"If I didn't have a lady..." Zach shook his head and took a drink.

"Yeah, right," I said. "You wouldn't hit on her in a million years."

"Hell yes, I would," Zach said. "I'm a good-looking guy."

"But you're intimidated by her," I argued. "You're telling me you would waste your time with her when she's squeezing Finn's bicep like that?"

Pepper took a long drink.

"I would try." Zach kept watching her. "What's the worst thing that could happen? She says no?"

"She *will* say no." I watched her get close to Finn, sharing a few laughs with him while they drank at the bar.

"You don't think I'm hot or what?" Zach rounded on me, genuinely offended.

"What?" I asked, disgusted by the question. "Of course I don't."

"What's wrong with me? You don't think I'm sexy?"

"Do you want me to think you're sexy?" I asked incredulously.

"Well, I don't want you to think I'm ugly." Zach forgot about Layla and just focused on me.

Pepper kept drinking.

"I don't think you're sexy," I said. "But I don't think you're ugly either. Alright?"

Zach still looked disappointed. "I guess I'll take it..."

I watched Finn pay for their drinks, and then they

walked out together. His arm circled her waist, and he escorted through the bar and out the main door. "Looks like you missed your chance. Finn's taking her home tonight."

Zach shook his head. "Lucky bastard."

Pepper turned her head and watched them go, her eyes wide with terror. Her fingers loosened on her glass, and her skin turned the color of milk. When they were gone, her eyes fell down once more.

Pepper had been weird all week, and now I wondered if her mood had anything to do with Finn. "Pepper? You alright?"

She didn't seem to hear me. "Excuse me, I need to use the restroom..." She left the table abruptly and walked away.

"What's that about?" Zach asked. "For one, the bathroom is way over there..."

I turned around and watched her go, seeing her step out the front doors and directly into the pouring rain. All this time, I thought I saw something between Pepper and Finn, but I was sure it was just paranoia. But now, I saw her storm outside like she had nowhere else to run, like seeing Finn with Layla hurt her so deeply she didn't know what else to do.

How had I not seen it before? "I'll be back."

"Where are you going?"

I left Zach's side and jogged through the bar to catch up with Pepper. I pushed through the doors and made it outside, getting hit with hard drops of rain right away. My eyes scanned the sidewalk and found her walking in her heels, the dress already soaked and revealing the contours of her flesh underneath.

I jogged to her side and stripped off my jacket. "Pepper."

She stopped in her tracks and turned to me, her makeup smeared from her tears, not the rain. Her mascara ran in rivers down her cheeks and to the corners of her mouth. With eyes red and puffy, she looked like she'd been sobbing rather shedding a few tears.

I pulled my jacket around her and zipped up the front, not wanting the world to see her wet tits in the thin material. "Pepper, talk to me." Now my clothes were soaking wet, but the cold didn't distract me. The agony on her face was like a thousand knives in my stomach. It was just like the night we signed our divorce papers, when she sobbed for the end of our marriage. I was being transported back in time.

She wiped the smeared mascara away, but more tears just kept coming. "I'm in love with Finn." The water fell hard on the sidewalk around us, making a loud cacophony of sound that diminished the sound of her voice. But her words still made it to my ears perfectly. "I'm so stupidly in love with him, and it fucking hurts. You're the person I tell everything to, and it's been killing me to keep this to myself. But now

I'm at rock bottom, and I just don't care anymore..."
She crossed her arms over her chest, clearly cold but
unwilling to get out of the rain.

My ex-wife just told me she was in love with my
brother, and I could barely process that reality. When
she dated Jax, all she wanted to do was keep him at a
distance. But now she said she'd fallen in love with
someone... It was so unexpected. It took me a minute
to accept what she said. "How? How is that possible?"
They'd spent some time together, but not enough to
warrant such strong feelings. How could Pepper fall in
love with my brother? A man whose last name she
shared?

"I don't know." She kept talking through her sobs.
"I don't even know when it happened. It just hit me
when he left. We've been seeing each other for the last
few months, and instead of it just being a fling, it
turned into something more...at least for me."

I felt like she'd punched me in the stomach.

When she realized what she'd admitted, she looked
apologetic. "I'm sorry, Colton. I didn't mean for you to
find out like this. I never meant to tell you. But you're
my best friend, and I need you right now. I'm heartbro-
ken, and I don't know what to do. Watching him walk
out with Layla nearly killed me..."

The sting of their betrayal hurt my heart. Now I felt
stupid for not noticing sooner, for being naïve around
both of them. I always thought I detected the chem-

istry, but I stupidly believed they would never fool around behind my back. But my anger didn't seem important when I looked at Pepper in that moment, seeing the heartbreak streaking down her cheeks. She was standing in the pouring rain, more distressed than I'd ever seen her in my life.

My feelings didn't matter.

She stared at me as she waited for a reaction, wiping her fingers underneath her eyes even though more rain hit her skin.

"It's okay."

She took a deep breath, and her eyes softened.

My arms circled her waist, and I held her close to me, letting her cry against my shoulder.

She squeezed me hard and released a shaking breath, clinging to me like that was exactly what she needed.

I was the reason Finn left with Layla that night. I was the reason Pepper was sobbing her heart out. I was the reason they weren't together—and I couldn't let that happen. I was hurt by the betrayal and I was uncomfortable by the relationship, but I wouldn't stand in their way. If this was what Pepper wanted, the woman I loved, then she could have it. "Then be with him."

She pulled away. "I can't. He ended things last week."

"Did he say why?" It was obvious that Pepper had

no idea Finn and I had talked about this. If she did, she would have confronted me sooner.

She sniffed. "Just said he didn't see it going anywhere..."

He did see it going somewhere. He said he wouldn't have asked for my permission unless he did. I was the obstacle standing in their way, the only thing keeping them apart. And Finn took the fall...to protect me.

AFTER I DROPPED off Pepper at her apartment and put her to bed, I returned home.

I hoped Finn was there—and not in bed with Layla.

I was greeted by Soldier when I walked inside, but I ignored him and headed into the kitchen.

Finn was there, drinking a glass of water at the counter with a bottle of Aleve beside him.

"Is Layla here?" I blurted, afraid she was upstairs and naked in his bed.

"No." He took another drink before setting the glass on the counter. "I told you I don't fuck colleagues."

"But you left with her."

"She was drunk and needed a ride home." He gripped the edge of the counter and sighed.

Now I understood his behavior for the last week.

He'd been moping around the house because he broke up with Pepper and let her believe he didn't want her anymore. He stopped shaving, stopped working out, and barely left the house unless it was for work. "You should tell Pepper that, because she assumed the worst."

His gaze shifted to my face.

I stepped closer to the counter. "She was upset when you left with Layla. I comforted her, and she told me everything."

He was still, holding his breath as he waited for my reaction.

"I'm not going to stand in the way if you want to be together. I want Pepper to be happy, and if you're the thing that makes her happy...my feelings shouldn't matter. I still think it's a terrible idea, but do what you want."

He straightened and dropped his hands from the counter. "Really?"

I nodded. "I love her more than anything in this world. It kills me to watch her cry."

He closed his eyes for a moment, as if that revelation hurt him.

"If you make her happy, keep making her happy."

He crossed his arms over his chest and breathed a sigh of relief. "I'm glad to hear you say that. I've been miserable without her."

"She's been miserable without you."

"Well...thank you."

I nodded.

"Are we okay, then?" he asked, gesturing between us. "Can we put this behind us?"

I wouldn't let my feelings get in the way of their relationship, but I couldn't pretend the betrayal didn't make me bleed to death. "You have my permission to be with her. But no, we aren't okay."

His eyes fell in sadness.

"I was mad when you asked for my permission to date her, but I got over it in a couple of days. It wasn't that big of a deal. But knowing you've been sneaking around behind my back and screwing my ex-wife..." I shook my head. "I can't forgive you for that."

He bowed his head.

"You lied when you asked for my permission. You don't need permission if you're already fucking."

"Colton—"

"Any other woman on the planet would have been fine, but you went after the woman I love, the woman I was married to, my best friend. She was the one person on this planet who was off-limits, but you did it anyway. I thought I saw the signs there was something going on between you two, but I always brushed it off because I knew you wouldn't betray me like that. We're brothers. But I was wrong...you made me into a fool."

"That's not how it was—"

"I'm moving in with Zach tomorrow. I'll stay there until my apartment opens up."

"Colton—"

"You made your decision." I turned away. "Now I've made mine."

ALSO BY E. L. TODD

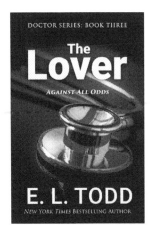

Against all odds, Finn and I have managed to be together.

Colton continues to warn me, says that Finn will never change.

But he already has.

I don't know what the future holds...but I think Finn fits in somewhere.

Order Now